ISBN-13: 978-1500799137

ISBN-10: 1500799130

Blake

Si Vis Pacem Para Bellum

NOTE FROM THE AUTHOR

The events in this story take place several years before Panic, the first novel in the Leopold Blake series of thrillers, and are loosely based around the financial crisis that hit the world in 2007.

Paydown is a short novel, and a classic prequel to the other books in the series, which can be read and enjoyed in any order. I've made sure not to include spoilers (for those of you who are new to the characters) and any existing fans of Leopold's escapades will still find plenty of fresh action and mystery, as well as a little background detail on some of the major players in the Leopold Blake universe. All in all, there's something for everyone.

I had an absolute blast writing this book - I hope you have a blast reading it too.

Nick Stephenson

For William

PAYDOWN

A Leopold Blake Thriller

SUMMER 2007

Leopold Blake sat in the hotel bar, two martinis already in him, and waited. A man in a tux played the piano in a far corner and the room was full, though Leopold had managed to find a stool near the taps. He helped himself to a handful of peanuts from the jar on the counter and caught the barman's eye.

"Same again?" The man cleared the empty glass away.

"Dry this time," said Leopold. "No peel. If I want lemon, I'll order lemonade."

The barman nodded and picked up a

shaker. Leopold watched him fill the steel container with ice before pouring in a healthy measure of Bombay Sapphire. Next, he dripped dry vermouth into a cold glass, swirled the liquid around the rim, and poured the contents away. He stirred the gin and strained it into the glass.

"Sir." The barman slid the drink over.

Leopold nodded and sipped. It was good enough, not perfect. The room felt warmer, probably thanks to the alcohol, and Leopold felt hungry. The peanuts didn't help, making him want to drink his martini all the faster, but his aim wasn't to get drunk, not tonight. Not while he was working.

Outside the barroom, near Reception, a woman marched across the floor. The clip clap of her heels on the polished tiles sounded a familiar gait, the right foot falling harder than the left, either a limp or ill-fitting shoes. Leopold figured the latter. A cop's salary didn't usually stretch to luxury footwear.

She reached the carpet, the sound of her approach vanishing just as the light hit her face. Her features were alluring, Leopold always thought, with her high cheekbones and sharp jaw. And the eyes.

Leopold stood up as she drew close, her perfume drifting into his nostrils. She wore a black dress, a clutch bag slung over one shoulder. The outfit looked brand new.

"Blake, you better have a damn good reason for dragging me out at this time of night," she said.

He glanced at his watch. "It's ten thirty p.m."

"Damn right. You know what time I get up?"

"We're here to surveil. We can't surveil someone while we're asleep, can we?"

"Are you drinking?" She eyed his half-empty glass.

"I'm blending in." He smiled and took another sip. "One for you?"

"I'm on duty."

"You strike me as a Bellini kind of girl." He turned and snapped his fingers. The barman had apparently overheard, fetching down a bottle of Moët from the fridge.

"I said no."

"Relax, Mary. We might be down here a

while."

"That's Detective Jordan to you, Blake. After what happened last time, make sure you behave yourself, or you might find yourself in more trouble than your high-priced lawyers can handle."

He raised one eyebrow. He liked it when Mary got mad. Her Brooklyn accent always broke through when she got riled up.

"I'll try to behave." Leopold slid her drink over. "At least hold on to it."

Mary obliged. "Any sign of the mark?"

"I saw him come through around eight. According to his calendar, he's due for drinks at eleven, meaning he'll resurface soon."

"I suppose I'd better not ask how you got access to his calendar."

Leopold smiled. "This guy does most of his best work outside the office. The VIP room at *Suave* is a regular haunt – bottle service usually gets the clients loosened up pretty fast. After that, it's back to the hotel for room service and paperwork until around three. Then he's back in the office for nine a.m."

"You've been tailing him a while, I see."

"It pays to be thorough." Leopold drained the last of his martini.

"Take it easy. We've got a long night. I need your..." she paused. "I need your particular *skills* as sharp as possible. You're no good to me half-asleep."

"I prefer to think of it as half-awake," he said, ordering a fourth cocktail. "And don't worry. Even with half my brain, I'm still smarter than anyone else in the room."

"And so modest, too."

"Modesty serves little purpose. Other than to feed one's insecurities by inviting more praise, that is. I have no need."

"No. You have an entirely different need." She eyed his fresh glass. "Just stay sharp, that's all. What else can you tell me about the mark?"

"Teddy Gordon's a Wall Street guy through and through. Private school followed by Princeton got him into all the right parties, landed him a job at Needham Brothers. Made senior analyst within a few years, then partner. He was bringing home five hundred grand a year plus the same again in bonuses before he hit thirty."

"Looks like I'm in the wrong profession," Mary said. She sighed in defeat and took a sip of the Bellini.

"Five years later and he's a senior VP, managing eight hundred million in client money. That's quite the ladder to climb in such a short time."

"You think he's working an angle?"

Leopold dropped a handful of peanuts into his mouth and chewed thoughtfully. "We're in the middle of a housing boom. It's been six years since the dot-com bubble burst and people are throwing their money around again. Downtown property values have risen eight percent a year for the last three years in a row. That kind of growth doesn't happen without a few people bending the rules. And Teddy Gordon keeps some interesting company." Another handful of nuts.

"You think Needham is turning a blind eye?"

"Undoubtedly."

"How do you know all this?"

Leopold shifted on his stool. "I had to get used to dealing with money at an early age.

Just as well, really. How many fifteen-year-olds inherit enough money to pay a small country's tax bill?"

"Poor you." Mary took another sip of her drink.

"Look, there are tricks you can play to manipulate the market. It's all based on perception. The money isn't real; the value of something is based solely on how much someone will pay for it, and that's controlled by how the buyer thinks everyone else is going to react. A smart banker understands how the buyer thinks, how the market thinks. He reacts accordingly."

"Yeah, you lost me."

"I'll give you an example. A bank gives some poor schmuck a mortgage at 100% the value of his property. No deposit. The bank sells the debt off to a larger bank in return for instant cash. The larger bank bundles up a hundred crappy mortgages like this and sells insurance policies for ten cents on the dollar – because their analysts tell them it's a sure thing. They do this with thousands of loans. The mortgage securities market grows. Nothing can go wrong, right?"

"Until the homeowner can't make his repayments."

"Right. Enough defaults, and it starts a chain reaction. The value of the house goes down, so the original bank can only reclaim 75% of the money. Or less. The larger bank who bought the debt is now on the hook for the insurance payout, and has to cover the full value of the mortgages they bundled together. They lose their cash reserves, meaning they stop lending. Or they go bust."

"And if nobody's lending, nobody's buying. Everybody loses."

"Yeah. Well, except for the guy buying up the insurance policies." He winked.

"It's an interesting theory. But what's this got to do with Teddy?"

"That's what we're here to find out. " He checked his watch again. "He's running late."

Mary put down her drink. "Maybe it's time we arranged a visit."

"What did you have in mind?"

The hotel elevator opened up into the hallway of the twentieth floor, offering a fine view of midtown Manhattan. The streets below were a blur of taillights, mostly taxis, and the nighttime sky was a muddy orange blur. The thick windows kept out most of the noise.

Mary pulled out a credit card. "He's in room 2037. We'll rattle the door, pretend we've got the wrong room. This should pass as a key card."

"And if he doesn't answer?"

She shrugged. "I'll have housekeeping drop by."

"It's not exactly covert," said Leopold.

"You give people far too much credit. Worse case scenario, he stiffs on the tip." Mary led the way down the long corridor until they reached Gordon's room. "Ready?"

Leopold nodded. "After you."

Mary rattled the handle and leaned her weight against the door. She jostled the handle again, louder this time. Leopold glanced down at the floor, noticing the strip of light under the door. If Gordon came to the peephole, he'd cast a shadow. Mary tried the handle a third time and swore, a little louder than was necessary. There was no movement from within.

"Is there another way out of the hotel?" she asked.

"Only for staff."

"Maybe he figured out we were tailing him and bolted."

Leopold shook his head. "He had no clue."

"We could have missed him. We'd better check downstairs."

"No. The lights are on inside. With these systems, they go out whenever you leave the room and take your key card with you."

"Maybe he forgot."

"Or maybe he's ignoring us."

Mary nodded and slipped her credit card back into her clutch. She pulled out her NYPD shield. "Okay. Looks like we might have to go find the manager."

After a heated argument with one of the hotel supervisors, Mary threatened to make a scene. The man acquiesced and sent them back upstairs with one of the housekeeping staff, an aging gentleman who smelled of pipe tobacco. He swiped open the lock and waved them through.

Mary pushed open the door slowly. Leopold saw her right hand drift down to her thigh, resting just above the hem of her dress. Now he was looking closer, he could make out a subtle bulge under the material. He had wondered where she was keeping her gun. Mary stepped through, as quietly as possible, and Leopold followed.

The hotel room was spacious, though modestly appointed. There was a small desk and seating area near the window. The view looked out toward Central Park a few blocks away, the treetops just visible. The room itself would have been unremarkable if it weren't for the smell; there was a sweet, sickly scent filling the air – like raw steak left out on the countertop to get warm. Leopold felt his stomach clench.

The mutilated body of Teddy Gordon was splayed out on the bed like a torn rag doll. Blood adorned the walls, what looked like arterial spray, a thicker pool forming on the sheets. Gordon's skin showed pale white where it wasn't soaked in red, a deep gash across his throat. There were several darker spots across the abdomen and the eyes were wide open, staring up at the ceiling. The housekeeper stepped through behind them and gagged.

"Dial 9-1-1," Mary said. "And tell your security team to seal off the exits. Whoever did this might still be in the hotel."

The doorman nodded and scampered away without a word.

"Blake, don't touch anything," she said, as Leopold noticed an ornate fountain pen lying on the desk.

"Relax." He walked over and leaned in, taking a closer look. "I know the protocol."

"You do when it suits you. Now just behave; I need to call this in. I can have a forensic team here in less than twenty minutes."

"What about our friend with the key? You told him to get the police on the phone."

Mary smiled. "I just needed him out of here. Whoever did this is long gone." She glanced down at the body. "I have to say, as far as surveillance operations go, this doesn't exactly rank in my top ten."

"Since when did you get mixed up with the fraud unit?" the tall detective eyed Mary, looking her outfit up and down. "They've been tailing this guy for weeks. Never found nothing. Then you show up and we got a corpse? Maybe I should haul you in." He laughed.

"You never heard of sharing resources?" she replied, arms folded. "Captain Oakes volunteered me."

"And him?" the detective jerked his head in Leopold's direction.

"Like I said. Sharing resources." She broke off the conversation and joined Leopold at the desk, leaving the detective alone next to the body on the bed. The forensic team was late.

"Friend of yours?" Leopold asked.

"That's Bullock. Works homicide with me. Thinks he's God's gift or something." She shrugged. "Though you've got to admit, it doesn't look good. We take over the case and the guy winds up dead."

"You called me, remember?" said Leopold. "Not that I don't appreciate the opportunity to lend a hand. You could certainly do with the help."

"Oh really? You're telling me this case has nothing to do with all the money you've got tied up at Gordon's firm?"

"Believe me, I could buy Needham Brothers twice over if I wanted. The money isn't a concern. What does worry me is what Gordon's doing with it."

"What he was doing with it." She glanced over at the body.

"Right."

"You got anything solid?"

"Not yet. Just strange things happening with the balance sheets; assets written down, or removed entirely. Inflated income reports, money filtering out of client accounts for a few days then suddenly reappearing. That sort of thing."

"You think he's using client money as his own?"

"That's the most likely explanation. If we can figure out who his other clients are, we can get access to their accounts too. See if the same thing happened to them."

"I'm guessing I shouldn't ask you too many questions about that."

"You learn fast." Leopold smiled. "Listen, I know people who can get information. It might not stand up in court…"

"It could get you arrested, more like."

"Only if someone tells on me." Leopold tapped his nose. "Whatever helps us get to the bottom of this has got to be a good thing, right? Gordon was murdered because he knew something. Or he was pissing off the wrong investors. Whatever the reason, it has to have something to do with his, shall we say, creative accounting."

Mary folded her arms. "I can buy that. Assuming you've got a shred of evidence he was mismanaging investors' money."

"I don't have anything you can use. Not unless you want to lose your job, that is." He fished a handkerchief out of his jacket pocket and used it to pick up the fountain pen he had seen earlier.

"Blake, what the hell are you doing? Put that down right now."

"Calm down. I won't get my prints on it. Besides, the forensic team isn't here. Who else is going to do their job for them?"

"Just put it back where you found it."

Leopold held up the pen. It was a Mont Blanc, black resin with an accented platinum clip. "A little chunky for my tastes, but bankers love them."

"What's your point?"

"You see any paper in here?"

Mary looked around.

"Gone. Along with his laptop and cell phone, no doubt. Which tells me whoever killed him was connected to at least one of the client accounts he was working on. Fortunately," he started unscrewing the pen,

"I think he kept a backup."

"What the – don't even think about…"

Leopold separated the two halves of the writing instrument, laying the nib section back on the desk. He held the other half up triumphantly. "Voila!" In his hand, a USB micro drive where the ink refill would normally be housed.

"You've got to be kidding," said Mary, peering closer. "How the hell did you know that was there."

"These pens are unusually thick and heavy. You know, phallic imagery and all that. The bigger the, um, pen, the bigger the… well, you get the idea."

Mary rolled her eyes. "Right, I forgot. It all comes down to dick measuring in the end."

"Exactly. So I wondered why this particular fountain pen is as light as a feather quill." He held it between thumb and forefinger, letting it dangle.

"Okay, I get the picture; it's a decoy pen. He was smart enough to keep a backup of all his data and hide it. So let's see what's on that thing."

"Oh, so now you want my help?" said

Leopold, grinning.

"Just shut up and go find a computer."

The USB drive was stuffed full of text documents, slide shows, and spreadsheets. Having requisitioned one of the hotel's many business suites, Leopold locked the door and punched a handful of search terms into the computer while Mary stood behind his chair, peering in. The hard drives whirred and spat out a few dozen relevant hits. He opened up a few files, scrolling through them with mounting disinterest, before finding something that caught his eye.

"Here, take a look at this." Leopold tilted the screen toward Mary.

"It's a bunch of numbers. Is this supposed to mean something to me?"

"These are tracking lists for a number of client accounts. Automated software can keep track of any number of stock prices, and these ones appear to be particularly important. See here," he traced his finger over the monitor, "Gordon kept these separate.""So?"

"So, this is how it looks if I put all the data in a graph." He clicked a few buttons and a line chart appeared.

"Wow, someone took a beating," Mary said.

"Quite. It's the same for all the others."

"They all bottomed out at roughly the same time. What would cause such a dramatic dive in value?"

"It could be any number of factors," said Leopold. "What's more important is why Gordon was keeping track of these accounts specifically. He's got historical data going back months."

"Maybe he knew what was going to happen. He could have made a fortune selling the stock short."

Leopold raised an eyebrow.

"What? Just because I'm a cop, I can't know about stuff like that?"

"I didn't say anything." He smiled. "You're

right, though; if someone knew the value of a company's shares was going to take a nosedive, he could make a killing."

"Probably not the most appropriate choice of words, considering the circumstances."

"We need to figure out who else had access to these accounts," he said, ignoring her. "Someone at the bank must have noticed what was going on. It can't be a coincidence that all these clients lost money in the same month."

"You're saying this is a cover-up?"

"It's the most logical assumption."

"Maybe we should go have a word with Teddy's boss," said Mary, making her way to the door. "You coming?"

"It's after midnight," said Leopold. "The managers go home in the evenings. The only people in the office at this time are low-level analysts. I doubt they'll be much help."

"Then go home," she said. "We'll drop by unannounced in the morning. Might surprise him enough to give something away." She left the room, closing the door behind her.

Leopold sighed and shut down the computer, pulling out the micro drive before getting up and heading for the door. Outside, the hallway was silent, any traces of the earlier commotion long gone, and the only sound accompanying Leopold as he walked to the elevators was the hum of the air conditioning. His mind whirred, poring over the facts of the case, trying to find a connection. The alcohol dulled his senses, reminding him he needed sleep. The answers would come soon enough, he assured himself. They always did.

Thirty floors below, the city marched on, oblivious.

Leopold got home a little after two thirty. One of the local bars, an upscale joint a few blocks from his apartment, was open late and Leopold had taken advantage. The staff knew him by name and had made his usual table ready. A few hits of bourbon had finished the night on a high note, and, with no further insights forthcoming, Leopold had resigned himself to a decent night's sleep and a fifty-fifty chance of a hangover.

His penthouse apartment was dark. The elevator opened up into the hallway, prompting the motion sensors to turn on the lights. It took a few seconds until a soft glow illuminated the ante room, then the living room and kitchen. Leopold tossed his jacket onto the coat rack and wandered through, heading for the armchair in front of the fireplace.

There was movement somewhere behind him and Leopold turned, a little too slow. A shadow moved fast, its shape blurred in the low light. Before he could move, the shadow was on him, blocking his path.

"What the hell?" Leopold stumbled, tripping over something on the floor. The main lights came on and he covered his eyes, squinting against the glare.

"It's late." The figure came into focus.

"Jerome? What are you doing up?"

"I'd ask you the same."

Leopold blinked hard and put down his hands. They were balled into fists.

"Were you planning on using those?" Jerome said, apparently amused.

"I get by."

"You missed training this morning."

"I was up early."

"How am I supposed to protect you if I don't know where you are?"

Leopold walked toward the armchair. "You're my bodyguard, not my nanny. It's your job to figure this stuff out." He dropped into the chair, feeling the soft leather envelope him. Sleep was near.

"That's not how it works." Jerome stalked over, crossing the room in two giant steps. He stood next to the fireplace and gazed down at his employer. "I'll chain you to the bed if I have to." At six feet seven inches tall and with the body of a pro wrestler, not many people argued with Jerome. His coal-black skin only intensified the look – clad in a finely tailored Armani suit and dark shirt, the bodyguard blended with the shadows perfectly.

"I'm touched," said Leopold. "Listen, I'll need you to take me downtown later this morning. I have an appointment at

Needham. We'll have company."

"The cop again?"

Leopold looked up. "You have a problem with Detective Jordan?"

"Not at all," said Jerome, a faint smile on his lips. "Though I'm guessing she might have a problem with you."

"She'll learn to live with it."

"It's late. You need to sleep."

"Then stop talking and leave me to it."

The bodyguard nodded and stepped away, leaving the room as silently as he had entered. Leopold took a moment to savor the emptiness of the room before leaning back in the armchair and closing his eyes. Within minutes, sleep was upon him, wrapping him tight like a soft blanket. Then the dreams came.

Leopold awoke early, just as the sun's rays broke through the litter of high-rises outside his window, and blinked hard. With a quiet groan, he forced himself out of the armchair and wandered over to his bedroom's bathroom, where he disrobed and threw himself into the shower.

Once dressed, he found Jerome waiting for him in the kitchen, a mug of steaming coffee in one hand. The bodyguard slid the drink across the polished marble countertop and Leopold caught it. He sipped, grateful for the caffeine boost.

"Assuming you're ready, I've asked for the car to be brought around," said Jerome. "We'll pick up Detective Jordan on the way."

Leopold smiled. "I don't see that happening, somehow. Mary left a message saying to meet us at Needham's."

"You're on first-name terms now, are you?"

"Don't get cute. It's far too early."

"You're the boss."

Once he'd finished his coffee, Leopold followed Jerome down to the lobby and out to the curb where a glossy black Mercedes waited. A uniformed doorman helped

Leopold into the back seat as the bodyguard got behind the wheel and started the engine. The V8 growled and Jerome pulled away, merging with the traffic heading south toward Seventh Avenue. They hit the FDR Drive and settled into a comfortable cruise.

"You gonna tell me a little about the case?" said Jerome, keeping his eyes on the road. "They got you doing anything good?"

"It started off as a fraud case, part of the NYPD's recent crackdowns. They set up a task force and apparently my connections to the finance world were judged to be an asset."

"Started off as a fraud case?"

Leopold shifted in his seat. "Yes. Suffice to say, things got a little more complicated last night after we found our lead suspect stabbed to death in his hotel room."

Jerome accelerated, overtaking a slow-moving truck. "You working murder cases now? I thought partnering with the NYPD was supposed to keep you out of trouble, not get you stuck in the middle of it."

"Relax. I can handle it. We're on our way to follow up a lead right now. You can tag along if you're worried."

"Who else is going to look after you?"

"Just try not to flash your gun at anyone. It tends to get them riled up."

The bodyguard grunted something in response.

Leopold grinned. "And let me do the talking, okay?"

———

Mary sat waiting for them in the reception lobby. She stood as they approached, holding out a thick manila folder. Leopold took it and leafed through the contents.

"This is everything?" he asked.

"Yeah. Autopsy won't come back for a few days, so I included the crime scene photos. Forensics didn't find much." Mary glanced at Jerome. "Brought some muscle this time?"

"Don't worry about him. He's here to make sure I behave myself."

"You've not learned how to do that yourself?"

"I've learned to, sure. I just don't find it much fun."

"We're not here to have fun, we're here to catch a killer."

"Yes, ma'am." He offered a mock salute. "By the way, how are we planning on getting inside?" He looked over toward the bank of elevators, flanked by a pair of burly security guards. "I don't think they appreciate walk-ins."

"That's what this is for." She fished out her NYPD shield.

"Put that away," Leopold put his hand over the badge. "Any of the staff notice there's a cop here, the whole building will be on alert. How's that supposed to help us?" He sighed. "Look, just follow my lead."

Leopold marched off toward the reception desk, beckoning the others to follow. The young blonde woman manning the phones looked up as he approached, flashing a set of brilliant white teeth.

"Can I help you?" she said, turning to face her visitors.

"Yes," said Leopold. "I need to speak with Teddy Gordon. Immediately."

"I'm very sorry, sir. But all appointments need to be made in advance. I'm afraid Mr. Gordon can't see you right now."

Leopold pulled a business card out of his jacket pocket and slid it across the desk. "I'm afraid it's urgent. Can you please call up and ask Mr. Gordon whether he can squeeze me in."

The receptionist glanced down at the card, maintaining her courteous smile. She typed something into her computer and Leopold noticed her expression shift almost immediately.

"I'm terribly sorry, Mr. Blake," she said. "I'll make sure somebody sees you right away. I'm afraid Mr. Gordon isn't contactable right now, but one of the senior vice presidents would be more than happy to talk with you."

"That will be fine, thank you."

The blonde held up three plastic key cards. "Here, these will grant you access to the thirtieth floor. Mr. Creed will meet you in the lobby."

Senior Vice President Vincent Creed was tall, very skinny, with closely cropped gray hair and a neat goatee. A well-tailored Astor and Black suit did a good job of bulking him out, but it could only go so far. The banker held out his hand as the trio drew close and Leopold shook it, surprised that Creed's grip almost crushed his palm.

"Good morning, Gentlemen. And Lady," said Creed, his dark eyes looking each of them up and down in turn. "Please, follow me to my office. This way."

The thirtieth floor was a maze of corridors, branching out to connect the bank's myriad departments into something resembling a cohesive whole. This floor, Leopold supposed, was designed to cater for the domestic efforts of their investment teams, based on the signage he could make out. Plaques above doors announced increasingly vague department names such as *Intra-Continental Growth Strategy* and *Internal Reliability Growth*. Creed kept up the pace and led them through to a waiting room at the end of the hallway, complete with receptionist, before pulling open a heavy glass door that opened up into a plush office.

"Come on through," the banker said, stepping inside.

Leopold followed, with Jerome and Mary close behind. The room was light and spacious, with wall-to-ceiling glass providing a decent view of the city. A large desk faced the door and Creed took a seat behind it, gesturing toward the seating area against the back wall.

"Please, make yourselves comfortable," said Creed, opening a drawer. He pulled out a glass decanter of amber liquid and four tumblers. "Can I offer anyone a drink? Single malt scotch, twenty years old."

Mary pulled out her police shield and held it up. "Not today. My name is Detective Jordan. I assume you know why we're here."

The banker eyed Mary warily before

relaxing and pouring himself a healthy measure of whisky. "It's an ancient tradition, toasting a fallen comrade." He raised the glass to his lips. "Terrible news. I got the call early this morning."

"Do you know of anyone who might have wanted to hurt Mr. Gordon?"

Creed ignored the question, turning his gaze upon Leopold. "So, Mr. Blake. How are you wrapped up in all this?"

"I'd answer the lady's question, if I were you," he replied. "She has a habit of getting what she wants. Eventually."

The banker straightened up and set his glass down on the desk. He stood and turned to face the window. "Teddy was a good man. A good worker. He looked after a great deal of money for our clients; he was always top tier. Teddy made a lot of people very rich, but there are always those who suffer as a consequence. It's part of life. Something that Teddy knew all too well."

"What do you mean?" asked Mary.

"There were threats. Nothing out of the ordinary. Some clients lose money; we can't win them all. The private investors sometimes get a little passionate about their portfolios." He sighed. "You have to understand, we take on a mix of clients. Teddy looked after mostly corporate accounts, but everyone takes a quota of private individuals looking to pad their retirement funds. Sometimes..." he trailed off. "Sometimes they don't get as much attention. They take it badly."

"Did anything specific happen to Mr. Gordon?"

"Teddy met his wife here at Needham," said Creed. "Did you know that? In this line of work, it pays to have someone at your back. Teddy did well to find his early. Helped him climb the ladder. Marriage isn't for everyone." He turned back to the desk and drained his glass. "But I digress. To answer your question: yes, there were threats. I'll have my secretary dig out the details."

"Tell me more about the wife," said Mary.

"Melissa Gordon," said Creed. "Nice enough girl. She had drive, that one. It's a shame really, what happened."

"Tell me."

"I'm guessing you're my first port of call, so to speak," he said, with a slight trace of amusement. "Well, I'm sure your due diligence would have turned it up anyway." He poured himself another drink. "Teddy and Melissa met a few years ago, working a buy side portfolio for one of the bank's up-and-coming accounts. They hit it off. She elected to take some time off after she got pregnant, but things didn't work out. Hit them both hard. Hit her worst of all. Her career took a nosedive. Teddy worked hard to try and make up for lost time. The man's a machine." He drained his drink once more. "Was a machine."

"They lost the baby?"

"Yes. And she was never the same afterwards. We ended up transferring her to a smaller office uptown, but she didn't like the idea. Eventually, she quit."

"What did this mean for Mr. Gordon?"

"Like I said, he worked hard to pick up the slack. Hell, it wasn't long before he was earning more than enough money on his own, but he kept on going. Unfortunately, at the expense of some of our smaller accounts."

"And these smaller investors got angry," said Mary. "Maybe wanted some answers?"

Creed sat down again. "Like I said, I'll have my secretary get the details for you. There was one guy in particular, used to show up at the office all the time. Briggs, I think his name was. Or Higgs. Something like that."

"Anything happen?"

"Yeah, it got pretty hairy on occasion. Guy tried to follow Teddy home once or twice. He denies it, but I wouldn't be surprised if they came to blows."

"We'll get the details from your assistant. Is there anything else you can tell us?"

"Nothing that comes to mind."

"Thank you, Mr. Creed." Mary stood up. "We'll see ourselves out."

The senior banker nodded curtly but remained seated, his gaze now fixed on the remnants of the scotch. Leopold knew the look well.

Vincent Creed was hiding something.

The secretary, a young man who introduced himself as Brian, handed them a printout of names and addresses after a few minutes of fiddling with his computer. The list contained a dozen entries, each with a short description, and Brian told them to work from the top down. Leopold had thanked him and stuffed the list into his jacket pocket, before leading the three of them back down to the lobby and outside onto the sidewalk. Jerome set off to retrieve the car.

"That's police evidence," said Mary, reaching out a hand. "Give it here."

"Not a chance," said Leopold. "You need me on this case, even if you don't know it yet. If I give you this, you'll try to shut me out. That would be a mistake."

"Don't flatter yourself. What the hell do you know about murder cases?"

"More than you think."

"Yeah? Like what?" She folded her arms, apparently annoyed at her own temper.

"Like Creed wasn't telling us everything."

"I know that, dumbass. I'm a cop. I can smell bullshit a mile away."

"That's not all. The photographs you took of the crime scene – did you happen to notice anything a little odd about the body?"

"I told you already, the autopsy won't be for a few days."

"I'm not talking about using the autopsy report," said Leopold. "I'm talking about using your eyes. Actually look at the photos." He pulled a full-page print from the manila folder under his arm and prodded the paper with an index finger. "Tell me, what do you see here?"

Mary took a step back. "What the hell are you talking about?"

"Tell me what you see. Come on, you said you were a cop. Cops have instinct, don't they?"

"Fine." She peered at the photo. "I see a dead guy with a bunch of stab wounds to the chest and a slit throat. So what?"

"So what does this tell you about the attacker?"

"That he had a knife."

Leopold sighed. "The cause of death was blood loss, thanks to the severed carotid arteries. When the killer slit Teddy's throat, the blood sprayed all over the walls here, and here." He pointed at the photo. "The blood pooling around the abdomen wounds suggests that he was alive when they were inflicted, but the lack of spreading suggests his blood pressure was very low. In short, he was practically dead already. So why would the killer stab someone who was already dying?"

"He might have wanted to make sure he'd done a good job."

"Sure, I can buy that. Except when the victim has six stab wounds, all inflicted after the death blow was already dealt and Teddy was practically unconscious. Not to mention the wounds are irregular in depth and spacing."

"So what? People freak out all the time."

"The cut to the throat was a precise and deliberate attack. The stab wounds are entirely the opposite."

"Get to the point."

"Whoever did this was someone who

knew Mr. Gordon personally. The killer would have harbored deep resentment toward Teddy – there's a definite connection between them. There's real hatred here. The killer enjoyed it."

"And you can tell me what the connection is?" Mary took a step forward.

"Well, no. Not right now, but –"

"Then shut up and let me do my job. Half-baked theories aren't going to help me get an arrest warrant, are they?"

Leopold slipped the photos back into the folder. "This doesn't change anything. I'm coming with you to interview the first name on this list." He patted his jacket.

"Fine. Just keep your opinions to yourself."

"Whatever you say."

Before Mary could respond, the Mercedes pulled up at the curb with a muffled growl. Jerome rolled down the front window and peered out. "Can we offer you a ride, Detective?"

Mary looked at Leopold. "I wouldn't want to put you to any trouble."

"Don't be silly," said Leopold. "How else

are you going to get there? You have no idea where you're going." He pulled open one of the rear doors and stepped to the side. "Go on, jump on in."

"You know, you could enjoy this a little less," she said, before letting out a deep sigh. "Let's just get it over with."

***

The first name on the list belonged to Joseph Biggs, his address listed in the Brownsville district of Brooklyn. Mary stared at the piece of paper, eyebrows raised. "This guy does business with Needham. Why is he living in one of the roughest areas in New York?" she said. "Even cops don't hang around here after dark."

"We'll find out soon enough," said Leopold. "Though I'd venture a guess that his investment portfolio probably didn't yield quite the returns he was looking for."

"We're nearly there," said Jerome, easing

the big car into a side road.

Leopold glanced out of the window. The bustle and glamor of Manhattan seemed a long way behind them now; the Brownsville neighborhood was largely deserted, only a handful of people out on the streets. Empty cars lined the roads. Most of the stores were closed, metal shutters blocking the insides from view.

"Here's the address," said Jerome. "We can pull in here." He steered the car onto the curb and down a wide alleyway, parking just out of sight. The door locks clicked open.

"This is the place?" Mary asked, climbing out of the back seat.

"According to this, yes." Leopold held up the list of names. "Apartment B. Sounds like a basement apartment."

"Great. Nothing better than confronting a potentially violent suspect when you've got no escape routes." She patted her hip instinctively.

"Relax. Just try not to wave that thing around." Leopold eyed the bulge of her firearm. "And keep that police shield to yourself. I don't think this is a registered neighborhood watch area."

"You can say that again."

Leopold glanced around as Jerome locked the car. Across the road a group of young men huddled around a wooden bench. Some were smoking, others handed around a brown paper bag with something inside, probably alcohol. A couple of others sat engrossed in their cell phones. The few pedestrians in the area gave them a wide berth.

"Cloccs," said Mary. "One of the smaller gangs. But they try to make up for it."

"Let's just hope they don't try anything stupid," said Leopold, glancing up at the bodyguard. "Lead the way."

The entrance to the apartment building looked out onto the alleyway. The door was reinforced steel, with a panel of buzzers mounted off to the side. Jerome jabbed the call button for Apartment B and waited. After a few seconds, he pressed it again. With a short burst of static, an irritated voice came on the line.

"Who the hell is this?" The voice was

male.

Mary stepped forward before Leopold could speak. "Mr. Biggs?" she said. "We're here to talk to you about Teddy Gordon."

Silence.

Mary tried a different approach. "We might have some news about your accounts at Needham. Can you let us in?"

Leopold heard a faint scuffle on the line and the door locks buzzed open. Mary pushed through into a darkened hallway and waved the others forward. Inside, the smell of stale cigarette smoke hung in the air, mingled with stale cooking smells. Chinese food. Curry. The stink of grease. At the end of the hallway an unmarked door led down a flight of steps to the basement. Apartments A and B were at the bottom. Mary knocked on Biggs' front door, one hand resting against her hip, just underneath her jacket.

The door opened a crack, the chain still attached. A pair of bloodshot eyes peered out.

"Mr. Biggs?" said Mary. "Can we come in?"

"Who are you?" said Biggs, his voice

scratchy. He looked and sounded like he hadn't slept in days.

"My name is Detective Jordan. I'm with the NYPD." She held up her shield. "We're here to talk to you about Teddy Gordon."

The door slammed shut.

"I told you to keep that thing to yourself," said Leopold. "How are we going to speak to him if he won't let us in?"

"What else was I supposed to do? It's standard procedure. I have to identify myself as a police officer, otherwise anything we get from him is inadmissible."

"You don't get it. We're not looking for admissible evidence, we're looking for a link to Teddy. We can find the evidence once we know where to look. And now we've hit a dead end. What do –"

He was cut off by a scrabbling sound from behind the door. The hinges creaked again and Biggs opened up. He stood in the doorway, dressed in shorts and a stained white vest that showed off an ornate tattoo across the shoulder and neck. A protruding gut and several days' stubble completed the look – classic white trash.

"You comin' in or what?" Biggs said, turning his back and heading for a tattered sofa in the corner of the room. He slumped onto the cushions and let out a burp.

"Erm, thanks," said Mary, stepping inside.

Leopold followed close behind. Biggs' apartment was a small studio, with a kitchenette and bedroom-slash-lounge taking up most of the space. Empty beer cans littered the carpet, which was stained and worn even without the fresh beer spills, and the sickly-sweet aroma of flavored tobacco permeated the atmosphere. Leopold noticed an empty pipe discarded on the coffee table, its burned-up contents tipped out into tiny piles of black ash. Jerome closed the door behind them.

"Can I get you something to drink?" asked Biggs, eyeing the insides of a crumpled beer can. He tipped it upside down and shook. Nothing came out.

"We're fine, thank you. Like I said, we're here to talk about Teddy Gordon. You were one of his clients, right?"

"Yeah."

Silence.

"Can you tell me about him? Were you happy with his work?"

"Yeah."

Silence.

"Mr. Biggs, we know you and Mr. Gordon argued about the money you had tied up in Needham. Can you tell me what happened?"

The man sighed, throwing the empty beer can to the floor. "Look, shit happens, right? I came into some money a few years back. Big lotto win. Blew most of it on coke and hookers, but a buddy of mine convinced me to invest whatever I had left."

"And how did that work out for you?" asked Mary.

"Went pretty good at first. Gordon promised me twenty percent in the first six months and the guy over-delivered. It was frickin' unbelievable. It's like the guy figured out how to print money or somethin'. After that," Biggs shrugged, "the shit hit the fan. Returns shrank. A year later and my investment's only worth half what I paid into the fund. As you can expect, I'm pretty frickin' upset."

"What did you do?"

"I went to see Gordon to ask him what the hell was going on. He blew me off, like I figured he would. Said he didn't look after the small funds no more. Said the market goes up and down, and there's nothin' can be done about it. Told me to file a complaint with his boss or take my money elsewhere. Not that there was much left at that point."

"How much?"

"Less than a hundred grand. I took the cash, blew it all. Wound up here. Like I said, shit happens."

"We have a witness who says you and Mr. Gordon fought. Thinks you and him might have come to blows once or twice. That ever happen?"

Biggs laughed. "You gotta be kiddin' me, lady. How the hell you think a guy like me is ever gonna get close enough to a guy like him? Not that I didn't occasionally fantasize about socking him in the face..."

"You could have followed him home. Gone to his office."

"What's the matter, you simple or something? Gordon had a driver take him home each night. Took him in mornings, too. Spent all day in the office. How the hell is a guy like me gonna get past that? I never even bothered trying to get an appointment. We spoke on the phone. That was it."

"You never met him in person?"

"I had a couple meetings early on, sure. But once the problems started, he didn't wanna give me the time of day. Told me to speak to his boss."

"Who was that?"

"Guy named Creed. Gordon said he was the one in charge of my account. Told me to take it up with him."

Leopold stepped forward. "Vincent Creed? He was the one managing your account, not Gordon?"

"You deaf? That's what I said. Gordon was the one bringing in the clients, laying the groundwork. Least, that's how he put it. Creed was the one managing the day-to-day. Seemed a little weird to me; the boss man running the accounts. Apparently, he only did that for a select few. Made me feel pretty good about the whole thing, 'til he messed it all up."

"And you're sure about this?"

"Of course I'm frickin' sure. You think I'd get forgetful about money, a man in my position? It might sound like small change to those Needham assholes, but it was everything I had." Biggs paused. "Why you here anyways? You got news about my money?"

Mary and Leopold looked at each other.

"Not exactly," said Mary. "We found Mr. Gordon's body late last night. He was murdered."

Biggs sat up. "Murdered? The guy's dead? Jeez, he was a scumbag but… hell. I'm never gonna see that money now, am I?"

"Your concern is touching. Can you think of anyone who might have wanted to hurt him?"

"You kidding? Probably every single person he ever screwed over. You got a pen and paper?" He laughed. "Might take a while."

"No, that's fine, Mr. Gordon. We have everything we need." She glanced at Leopold and flicked her eyes toward the door. "We'll see ourselves out."

Biggs belched and slumped even further down the sofa. "Pleasure meetin' you."

"Looks like we'll need to pay Mr. Creed another visit," said Leopold, as the three of them made their way back up the stairs. "I knew he was hiding something."

Mary pushed open the door into the hallway. "It's nearly lunchtime. Do these bankers ever go out to eat?"

"That's where they do most of their business. A guy like Creed would probably be meeting clients somewhere expensive. On company money, of course."

"Of course."

"I'll ask my contact to check Creed's schedule for the day."

"I'm guessing this is another one of those times I shouldn't ask questions."

"See, I knew you'd get the hang of this working relationship," said Leopold. "We'll surprise Mr. Creed at lunch, catch him off guard." He pushed open the steel door that led out to the alley and headed for the car.

As they rounded the corner, Leopold froze. The gang of young men he had noticed earlier had apparently taken an interest in his Mercedes – six of them were now inspecting the vehicle, taking it in turns to peer through the glass and test the doors. One of them looked up as Leopold, Mary, and Jerome approached.

"Hey, hey, what we got here?" the apparent ring leader shouted. His voice was deep and cocky, the hood of his coat pulled over his head. "Sweet ride. How much this cost you?" He turned to his companions and laughed. "Thinkin' bout gettin' me one of these. Needs a paint job, though. Maybe some new rims." He rapped the windscreen with his knuckle.

"Let me call backup," said Mary, her voice a whisper. "Don't engage. We don't know if they're armed."

"Of course they're armed," said Leopold. "But that doesn't mean they get to mess with my car."

"I think it does, actually."

"Maybe where you come from."

"We both come from New York."

"You know what I mean." Leopold looked up at Jerome. "Any ideas?"

The bodyguard looked at the gang of men. "Just stay behind me and don't speak. Things always get much worse when you speak."

Leopold considered a response, but too late. Jerome strode over to the hooded leader, closing the distance remarkably fast. The young man stood tall, chest puffed out, and met Jerome head on.

"You got somethin' to say, homes?" the kid said.

"Step away from the car."

"You gonna make me, big man? 'Cos last time I checked, there's six of us and three of you. One, two, three." The hood prodded Jerome with an index finger, emphasizing his point.

Leopold turned to Mary. "That wasn't a good idea," he said.

Too fast for the gang leader to react, Jerome grabbed hold of the finger prodding him in the chest and wrenched it backward. There was a cracking sound and the kid yelped, eyes wide, his bravado gone. Jerome twisted the finger to the side and pulled, forcing the arm to hyperextend. The kid turned to compensate and Jerome pulled him in close, a thick forearm across the throat. The other five gang members twitched nervously, their leader held fast in the bodyguard's grip.

"This would be your opportunity to leave," he said, still holding onto his opponent's finger.

The other gang members looked at one another, shuffling their feet. Nobody spoke. Jerome sighed and gave the leader's broken finger another twist. The young man screamed, the pain now clearly beyond anything he could handle.

"Leave, right now," said Jerome, "or I'll pull his finger off. And after that, I'll move on to the rest of you. I'd be lying if I said a part of me wouldn't enjoy that. But I'm afraid we're pressed for time, so I'll just have to shoot you." He let go of the finger and released his hold on the kid's throat. The kid dropped to his knees. With practiced speed, Jerome pulled out the firearm holstered beneath his jacket and pointed it at the closest of the other gang members.

"All right, all right." The new target held his palms up and backed away. "We're goin'. Just don't shoot."

Jerome pressed his foot against the leader's back and shoved him forward. "Take this with you," he said, keeping his gun up.

The kid got to his feet and scrambled away to join his companions, cradling his broken finger as he went. Within a few seconds the gang had disappeared around the corner and Jerome holstered his weapon.

"Okay, we can go now," he said, unlocking the car. "Apologies for the delay."

Creed's restaurant of choice nestled between a hair salon and clothing store. The sign outside boasted "A Fusion of East and

West" and the tables were packed full of people in suits ordering lunch from oversized menus. Leopold pushed open the heavy glass doors and stepped inside, the smells from the kitchen hitting his nostrils immediately. The interior was all glass and chrome and leather.

"This place smells kinda funky," said Mary, following behind.

"It's called fusion food," said Leopold. "It's undergoing something of a resurgence at the moment. The chefs take two different cuisines and blend them into something new."

"Just like Reese's did with peanut butter and chocolate." She chuckled to herself and picked up a menu. "Whoa, Jesus, I think I'd better stick with the candy after all. What the hell is with these prices? And why do they need such a big menu? There's only like five dishes to choose from." She squinted at the tiny italic text. "What exactly is grilled ahi?"

Leopold sighed. "We're in the middle of the financial district. The clientele have a lot of money to spend. Speaking of which, I think I see our man." He pointed across the room toward the back corner where Creed sat at a large table with half a dozen lunch guests. "How about we go say hello?" He took a step toward the dining area.

"Do you have a reservation, sir?" a maître d' dressed in a crisp suit appeared out of nowhere, blocking the way.

Leopold stopped in his tracks. "We're not here for lunch. I need to speak with a gentlemen at that table." He pointed.

"I'm sorry sir, our diners value their privacy. We can't allow anyone through without a table reservation."

"Then can I make one?"

"For today?"

"Yes."

"No."

"No?"

"I'm sorry, sir," said the maître d'. "We are fully booked for the next two weeks. Would you perhaps like to make a booking for next month?"

"No, I don't want to come back next month," snapped Leopold. "I want to speak to that man over there."

"I'm sorry sir, but – "

Mary interrupted, pushing her way past Leopold. She held up her NYPD shield. "Listen. Either you let us through or I book you on an obstruction of justice charge. How does that sound?"

The maître d' glanced at the shield. His expression relaxed a little. "Given the circumstances," he said, straightening his tie. "I'm sure I can make an exception. Please," he stepped to the side, "go on through."

Leopold brushed past without a word and headed for Creed's table. The senior banker was engrossed in a heated conversation with the other diners that Leopold couldn't make out. As he drew closer, Creed noticed and halted the conversation. The banker got to his feet and left the table, drawing Leopold just out of earshot of his companions.

"Can I help you, Mr. Blake?" he said, keeping his voice low. "I'm in the middle of a meeting." He spotted Mary and nodded. "Detective Jordan. A pleasure, as always. Where's your big friend?"

"He's in the car," said Leopold. "He never did like fusion food."

"Me neither, I'm afraid," Creed said. "But

these guys seem to. God knows why. It's all sushi as far as I'm concerned. Now, what is it I can do for you? I really must get back."

"We spoke with Biggs, the man you said had assaulted Mr. Gordon."

"Good. And he was of some help?"

"Yes. Though he said that Gordon wasn't the one looking after his account. He said that you were. He believes you're responsible for the loss of his fortune."

Creed's calm expression flickered momentarily. "Look, this really isn't a good time. I dealt with a lot of accounts, we all do. I already told you everything I know about Gordon. Now, if you'll excuse me, I have an important account on the hook here. It's not going to reel itself in."

"Mr. Creed..."

"Mr. Blake, if you need to speak with me again, either set up an appointment with my assistant or get yourself an arrest warrant. Now please excuse me." He turned around and walked back to his table, slipping back into his chair just as his lunch arrived. "You think we can get a warrant?" said Leopold.

"Based on what?" said Mary. "The guy's an

asshole, and he's definitely not telling us everything, but we can't get a judge to sign off without some hard evidence."

"We'll just have to go dig some up. There must be someone out there who dislikes Creed enough to talk to us about what goes on at the bank. Someone who works with him, maybe."

"Or worked. Preferably someone with a grudge. How do we narrow that down? There must be hundreds."

Leopold grinned. "I know exactly who can help." He turned and marched back toward the door. "Follow me."

The brownstone home of Teddy and Melissa Gordon was situated in one of the leafier parts of the Upper East Side, squeezed in between two other identical buildings about halfway down one of the many pristine side streets. Jerome rolled the

Mercedes up to the curb and killed the engine.

"Nice place," said Mary, looking out the window. "Don't you live around here?"

"I have an apartment, yes," said Leopold. "Closer to the park."

"What's the matter? Couldn't afford a real house?"

"Let's try to stay focused, shall we?" he said, opening the door and stepping out onto the sidewalk.

"No need to be so sensitive." She followed suit and joined Leopold outside. Jerome waited in the car.

"I'm guessing we won't have to worry about the Mercedes around here," said Mary. "The other cars parked out here are worth at least twice as much as yours."

Leopold rolled his eyes. "Are you determined to get some kind of reaction from me?"

"Oh calm down. You can be such a baby."

"Can we just get this over with? Creed is going to be on the defensive now, so time is short. We need to find something solid to link him to Gordon's murder. If he was really trying to sabotage his investors and Gordon found out, that's as good a reason as any. Hopefully Mrs. Gordon can help with that." He walked up to the door and rang the bell. "Otherwise we're back to square one."

"I'm just saying, you don't have to get all sensitive."

"I'm not sensitive, but that doesn't mean I have the patience to pretend your little remarks aren't getting annoying. Why don't you just spit it out? You clearly have something to say."

Mary opened her mouth to reply but was interrupted by the sound of the intercom crackling into life.

"Gordon residence. Mrs. Gordon isn't taking visitors, I'm afraid," the disembodied voice said. "Kindly call her assistant to set up a meeting for another day."

Leopold leaned in to the microphone. "I'm afraid it's imperative that we speak with Mrs. Gordon today. Right now, actually. We have some important news regarding Mr. Gordon's estate."

Mary shot him a fierce look.

Leopold ignored her. "We need to go over the details immediately."

There was a brief pause.

"Please wait there," said the voice. The line went dead.

"What the hell are you doing?" said Mary. "We're not here to talk about the estate. The minute she finds out we lied…"

"By that time, it won't matter. I had to say something to get us inside, and if you whip out that damn badge she's only going to be on the defensive."

"I'm required to identify myself as a police officer. And, if you want any of the testimony from Mrs. Gordon to be worth a damn in future, you have to identify yourself as a consultant for the NYPD. Otherwise we're wasting our time."

"Relax. I only need a few seconds. You can tell her what you want after that."

Mary sighed. "Fine. Just try not to get us into any trouble."

The intercom buzzed and Leopold heard the locks disengage. The door swung inward, revealing a tall man dressed in a butler's uniform. The man stepped to the side and waved them inside.

"Please, follow me. Mrs. Gordon will meet you in the drawing room." The butler led them through to a spacious room toward the back of the house, complete with high ceilings and neoclassical furniture – delicate tables, cabinets, and chairs with finely crafted tapered detail and gold leaf accents. The floors were polished marble, the walls clad with bold wooden panels. The room would not have looked out of place in the Palace of Versailles. A woman, presumably Mrs. Gordon, sat attentively on the sofa. She got to her feet as Leopold and Mary were ushered through.

"Good afternoon," she said, a weak smile forcing its way onto her lips. "Please, take a seat." She indicated two armchairs opposite her.

Leopold settled into his seat. "I'm afraid I must confess we're not here to talk about Mr. Gordon's estate. We're here to talk about who killed him." He paused. "What can you tell me about Vincent Creed?"

Melissa Gordon flinched. "Who are you people?"

"Ma'am, we're with the NYPD," said Mary, holding up her ID. "I'm Detective Jordan, this is Leopold Blake. He's a consultant."

Mrs. Gordon took a moment to let the words sink in.

"I know this must be difficult for you, ma'am…"

"You know nothing of the sort, Detective," she said, taking a seat. "My husband was a good man. He didn't deserve to die. I would advise not trying to empathize with me right now."

Mary nodded. "I understand, ma'am. We're very sorry for your loss. Did you know of anyone who might have wanted to hurt him?"

"He was a successful man. A lot of that success came at the expense of other people. But that's just business. I can think of dozens who would hold a grudge, but that's no different from any other successful trader. You've met Mr. Creed, I assume?"

"Yes, ma'am."

She smiled. "Then you know what I mean. He's hardly one to give off an aura of amiability, wouldn't you agree?"

Mary shifted in her seat. "I wouldn't know, ma'am. Did you and Mr. Creed know each other well?"

"Oh yes," she leaned back and folded her arms. "My husband and I actually met while we both worked at Needham, did you know that? After a few years, we started working in Creed's division and I took time out to have children." She paused. "As you can probably tell, that didn't work out. I was forced out of the firm not long after. Thankfully, Teddy managed to keep things going by himself. He always was a hard worker."

"Did any of your husband's clients express any negative feelings toward him?" asked Mary.

"He never spoke about work; I think he felt it might upset me. He would sometimes work from home, but most of the time he was at the office. He liked to keep his personal and professional lives separate."

"Did he keep a workspace here?" said Leopold, leaning forward.

"Yes, he had a study just down the hall."

"May we take a look?" He stood up. "There might be something we can use to figure out whether anyone at Needham might have been involved. Mr. Creed wasn't exactly forthcoming in that respect."

"I'm not sure my husband's private business is something I'm comfortable you seeing."

Leopold sighed. "His private business is what got him killed, Mrs. Gordon. If there's something about this case I know for sure, it's that somebody's not telling me everything. There's someone at Needham working to keep a secret and I'm going to find out what that is. Do you really want to stand in the way of that?"

Melissa Gordon's features darkened. "You dare come into my house…"

"We came into your house because your husband was murdered. Killed because he knew something he shouldn't. And somebody at your husband's firm is very probably involved in covering it up."

Mrs. Gordon stood up, shaking slightly. "Fine. You win. Follow me." She led them through to the hallway. "It's in here." She opened a thick wooden door to reveal a cozy room filled with bookshelves. Against the far wall a messy desk spanned most of the width of the floor, piled high with papers and old copies of the *Financial Times*. A slim computer monitor peeked out above the sea of clutter.

"I haven't touched it since he was last in here," she said. "Perhaps I'd better clear some things away."

Leopold leaned in and located the keyboard. He tapped the space bar and the screen burst into life. "Password?" he said.

"Try 'PLUTUS999'. All capitals."

He typed the letters. "Thank you. Here we are." The operating system loaded. Leopold reached up and tilted the monitor, keeping his hand on the frame. "Viewing angle is a little messed up."

"What are you looking for?"

"I'm not sure yet." He clicked on a few folders. "There must be thousands of spreadsheets and presentations on here."

"That's pretty much what an investment banker does," said Mrs. Gordon. "Push numbers around, make pretty graphs, and hope to hell whoever came up with the formulas knew what they were doing."

Leopold chuckled. "Sounds like a blast. Do you mind if I print a copy of this?" He brought up a text document detailing a list of historic transactions.

She squinted at the screen. "Sure, suit yourself. The printer's there."

"Thank you so much for your help." He fished the printed document from the tray and folded it, slipping it into his pocket. "I think we have everything we need. We'll be in touch soon."

As Melissa Gordon's butler closed the front door behind them, Leopold caught Mary's expression.

"What?" he asked, heading for the car.

"You did something I'm not going to like, didn't you?"

"I have no idea what you mean."

"Spill. I'll only figure it out eventually."

Leopold grinned, pulling an ornate Mont Blanc fountain pen from his jacket pocket. "Let's just say this case has given me a few good ideas." He unscrewed the nib to reveal a USB micro drive.

"You weren't supposed to take that," said Mary. "It's evidence in a murder case."

"Relax. We got all the pertinent information off it already. I was able to slip it into the port in the computer monitor. Copied over most of Teddy's work files. I used the printout to hide the pen as I slipped it back into my jacket." He grinned again. "We'll be able to take a proper look without Mrs. Gordon peering over our shoulders."

"Don't look so pleased with yourself." She opened the car door and climbed inside. "None of what we find is going to be admissible without a warrant. Just hope to God nobody finds out."

"Well, I'm not going to tell anyone." Leopold climbed into the front passenger seat. "And I don't think Jerome is going to tell anyone."

The bodyguard shook his head slowly.

"Good. Then I believe the only person who might cause any problems is sitting in the back seat."

"Just take me back to the station."

"Not a chance," said Leopold. "I'm

starving. I think it's time you and I had a little lunch date."

"They better serve real food in here," said Mary, eyeing up Leopold's choice of restaurant. "I've got no patience with tiny portions and giant plates."

The sign above the door to Mama Leone's boasted "New York City's Best" and Leopold knew it to be true. What the place lacked in sophistication, it more than made up for with authentic food and a thriving atmosphere. Leopold pushed through the door and the smell of cooking hit him immediately – roasted meats, scented oils, garlic, herbs, chopped tomatoes – making his stomach growl even louder. A waiter greeted them by the door and showed them to a cozy table for two near the window.

"Unfortunately, this place doesn't have wi-fi," said Leopold, settling into his seat and pulling out the laptop he had brought from the car. "But we should at least be able to check through the contents of Teddy's hard drive while we eat."

"Speaking of which," said Mary, "what's good here?"

"Everything's good. They'll bring the food over as soon as it's done, so they shouldn't be long."

"I haven't even ordered."

"It's best not to choose for yourself; you'll only get it wrong," he said, slipping the micro drive into the laptop's USB port. "They'll bring over whatever is freshest. Their menu is based on what they could get their hands on at the markets earlier in the morning. Trust me, it's better this way."

"I'd rather just have a cheeseburger."

"Just stop complaining and live a little." Leopold tapped a few keys and the laptop started to whir. "Good. The contents are all copied over, so all we need to do is find something that links Creed to all this."

"You really think he's behind this? I mean, my gut's telling me he's scum, but is he capable of murder?"

"I know he's hiding something." He opened a search and typed in a few keywords. "We're looking for anything covering the last few months' numbers. Anything that shows a steep drop in share value."

"Like we saw at the hotel?"

"Exactly. Here, look at this." He turned the laptop around to face her. "Consolidated accounts for the firm's top earners. See anything unusual?"

She peered in. "No. Should I?"

"That's just it. Where some of the share value of the smaller clients dropped through the floor, these stayed constant."

"So?"

"So, in any given week, the investment analysts allow for a variability of up to fifteen percent. They expect around five percent in a bad week, maybe one or two percent on an average one. Either way, it's up and down. These numbers are showing a constant growth. A perfectly straight line. Real life just doesn't work like that."

"Someone's cooking the numbers."

"Right. There's no way millions of dollars

can drop off the accounts of a select few accounts, while the top earners show zero volatility. Someone's taking one company's losses and turning it into another company's profits, making everything add up nicely."

"Gordon was behind this?"

"These aren't Teddy's accounts," said Leopold. "According to Biggs, Creed was the one overseeing the management. Teddy was the one bringing in the business. He wouldn't have had any idea."

"So why have all this on his computer?"

"Maybe he found something that didn't add up. Maybe that's what got him killed. But right now, there are more important things to focus on."

"Like what?"

"Like lunch," said Leopold, as the waiter arrived with two plates of steaming food. Leopold shut the laptop and stashed it under his chair.

"Buon appetito," the waiter said, laying the plates on the table.

The first dish was gnocchi sautéed in butter and olive oil, with pesto, sprinkled with parmigiano-reggiano, and accompanied by a fresh salad. The hot salty dumplings made a fine contrast to the crispness of the salad, and both Leopold and Mary finished their portions after a few hungry mouthfuls. The food kept coming – roasted sea bass with chili tomato sauce, lamb skewers marinated in garlic oil, scrambled eggs with brie, walnuts, and white truffle – Leopold drank red wine, a rich sangiovese, while Mary sipped club soda. Both ate everything, mopping up remaining sauce with hunks of herby ciabatta. For dessert, the waiter brought them tiramisu and espresso.

"I couldn't eat another bite," said Mary after taking the last morsel of bread, hand on stomach. "I think you've killed me."

"Take your time. The coffee will help you digest." Leopold tipped the espresso down his throat.

"We need to find something linking Creed to Teddy Gordon's murder. We don't have time to digest."

"Food is a kind of meditation. Your mind is focused on just one thing – eating. This allows your subconscious to churn away in the background on less exciting things."

"Murder cases not exciting enough for you?" said Mary, sipping her coffee.

"I thought there would be more action. You know, maybe a car chase or something. You think we can fit one in?"

"We can only hope."

Leopold smiled and shook his head. "Look, we have Biggs' testimony to work with. We can probably lean on Mrs. Gordon to back us up. And we've got these accounts on Teddy's hard drive. I'm betting they're on Creed's hard drive too."

"That's not enough to make an arrest. We need probable cause."

"I'm not finished. Take a look at the metadata in these files." He pulled out the laptop again.

"The what?"

"Every file is stamped with information about who owns the document, when it was created, and when it was modified. According to this," he opened up the spreadsheet again, "the records were created three months ago and were modified in the last forty-eight hours. More importantly," he turned the computer around and tapped the screen, "Creed's name is listed as the author."

"That still doesn't link him to the murder."

"No. But it should get you a warrant to search his computer. All you need is something giving him a motive. Maybe Gordon found out what he was doing, threatened to go public."

"Okay, we can work with that." Mary fished out her cell phone from her purse. She paused. "Wait a minute. If Creed was responsible for Gordon's death, wouldn't he have been at the hotel that night? We can check the security footage. If we can place him at the crime scene, we'll have motive, means, and opportunity. That'll get us our arrest warrant."

"Now you're talking," said Leopold. "I told you lunch was a good idea."

Creed came quietly enough. Halfway

through a suit fitting in his office, Mary had presented him with a choice: either come along willingly, or face the walk of shame in front of an office full of subordinates. Creed had chosen wisely.

Following a brief wait at the station for the man's lawyer, Mary had interviewed Vincent Creed to little result. The banker had remained silent throughout, speaking only to recite his name, address, and occupation. Mary had informed him of his rights and sent him down to the holding cells. Leopold had been told to wait outside.

"Are you done yet?" Leopold asked, as Mary stormed back into the waiting room. "The coffee here is terrible."

"I'm sure you'll survive a little longer," she said.

"He's been down in the cells for nearly an hour. What else do you expect to achieve by stomping around? His lawyer will be working to put a moratorium on any warrants to search Creed's computers, so make sure you get there first. You can hardly expect the man to confess without putting a little pressure on him."

"I know, I know. He just gets me riled up, that's all. Entitled bastard. You should have seen the smirk on his face all the way through the interview. Like he knew I couldn't do anything."

"You'll just have to prove him wrong."

"We don't have long. I need to officially charge him with something in the next five hours or he'll walk. And that's not going to happen without something a little more concrete to link him to the murder."

"You get his bank accounts?"

"Yeah. I've got some people going through them right now."

"Let's go take a look."

She hesitated, then let out a sigh. "Okay, fine. You can come; just don't speak to anyone, okay?"

"Wouldn't dream of it."

Mary swiped her ID card across the magnetic strip near the steel door at the back of the room. "And don't touch anything."

The three-man tech team was sifting through Creed's banking records as Leopold and Mary entered the room. Their office was small and dark, no windows and no natural light, and it smelled dusty. They clearly didn't get out much.

"What you got for me, boys?" said Mary, eying up the computer monitors.

The largest of the three turned his head. "We got a whole lotta numbers, that's what. This guy's frickin' loaded. A couple of transactions stand out though." He pointed at the screen. "Check it. There was a large cash withdrawal a couple days ago from five different ATMs downtown. Just a few blocks from the hotel Gordon was killed."

"That's a good start. We got him on the CCTV tapes, maybe he paid someone off."

"Yeah, maybe. We also got a large deposit, well, larger than usual, made into his account just this morning. Two hundred thousand dollars."

"Who made the payment?"

"We don't know," said the tech. "It's not from a US bank. Hell, we have no idea where it came from. It's gonna take us a few days to trace."

"Get on it," said Mary. "In the meantime, this is enough to at least get the assistant DA to sign off on an official charge. We can hold him downstairs until the bail hearing. That gives us time to assemble a case. Good work boys." She smiled.

"Ma'am." The big guy smiled back before returning to his workstation.

"I'll have some friends of mine check the bank account routing numbers," said Leopold, firing off a text message on his cell phone as they left the room. "Shouldn't take them long."

"Just keep me out of it," said Mary. "If you find any evidence we can't use it directly. And I don't want to know where it came from."

"Agreed. We should have an answer soon. In the meantime, let's go see Creed's lawyer. See what he has to say about all this."

Creed's lawyer was unimpressed. "None of this links my client to the murder," he said, getting up from behind the interview table. "You're clutching at straws. Let Mr. Creed go and stop wasting everybody's time."

"Sit down, Mr. Osborne," said Mary. "What we have is CCTV camera footage of your client at the scene of the murder. We have sensitive information exchanged between your client and the victim just hours before his death. We've also got a considerable amount of money deposited into Mr. Creed's bank account shortly after Mr. Gordon was killed. That's more than enough to file charges. Mr. Creed's not going anywhere. I suggest you inform him."

The lawyer picked up his suitcase. "You can expect me to fight this," he said. "And if you think I won't get bail, you're very much mistaken." He breezed out of the room without another word.

"God, I hate lawyers," said Mary.

"Who doesn't?" said Leopold.

Mr. Osborne returned less than twenty minutes later to find Mary and Leopold waiting for him outside the interview room.

"You done?" asked Mary.

"My client has been informed of the charges. When's the bail hearing?"

"Judge Robertson, Monday morning."

"I need to formally request the duty officer grant pretrial leave. Mr. Creed can be released on his own recognizance until then."

"I'll pass the request on. It will be denied."

"Please send the confirmation to my office. I'll see you in court." The lawyer marched off, disappearing around the corner.

"I'm guessing Creed didn't take the news too well," said Leopold. "Maybe we should go find out how he's doing."

"We can't. It would be ex parte," said

Mary. "We can't speak to him without his lawyer."

"Bullshit. We can speak to whomever we like. You need to loosen up a little. Come on, you said you needed more evidence – let's go get some."

The guard looking after the cells signed them in and led them through to the holding area. "You guys know his lawyer just left, right?" he said, fiddling with a giant set of keys.

"Yeah, we got it Jimmy," said Mary. "Anyone else been down?"

"Just the guy bringing chow. The boys should have finished by now. Go on through." He swung the heavy iron gate open and ushered them over the threshold. He followed, locking it behind him. "Just a couple more."

After a few minutes, they reached the

holding cells. The harsh neon lighting bounced off the white walls and floors, making Leopold squint. With no windows and the air conditioning shut off, the air in the room was thick with the smell of food. There were eight cells in total, each with solid metal doors. Jimmy the guard walked up to the farthest right and rapped a knuckle on the steel.

"Hey, yo. You got visitors," he said.

No reply.

"Open it up, Jimmy," said Mary, stepping forward. "You can wait for us outside, it's not a problem."

"Ma'am." He nodded and slipped a key into the door lock. "Here you go." He swung the door open.

"Good evening, Mr. Creed," said Mary, stepping toward the empty cell. "You enjoying your stay at –" She stopped mid-sentence.

"Holy shit," said Jimmy.

Leopold ran forward and peered past the others. Vincent Creed was slumped against the wall, his skin as white as porcelain, with one half of a prison fork protruding from his throat – his own hand still wrapped around the handle. Both carotid arteries appeared to have been punctured from several jabs to the soft flesh. There were dark bruises around the wounds, though there was very little blood on the body. Most of it had sprayed across the room and was dripping down the opposite wall.

"Holy shit," Jimmy repeated. "What the hell happened?"

"You tell me," said Mary. "You were supposed to be watching."

Leopold pushed through and knelt by the body.

Jimmy held up his hands. "I can't watch everyone at once, can I? I got other work to do, I can't be expected –"

"Keep quiet, both of you," said Leopold. "Who has had access to this cell today?"

"Just the guy's lawyer. And the other guy bringing food. Damn, how the hell he do that with a spork?"

Leopold noticed something on the floor and bent down for a closer look. "Plastic shards. The cutlery was snapped in two, with one end filed down into a point against the wall."

"Jesus."

"And who said anything about him doing this to himself?"

"What, you think someone else broke in and killed him with a spork?" Mary said. "I don't see any signs of a struggle here. No defensive wounds. The guy knew we were on to him; maybe prison was too much for him to face. It's not unheard-of."

Leopold sniffed the air. "What's that smell?"

"What smell?"

He turned to Jimmy. "You let people smoke in here?"

"Not since Bloomberg's witch hunt. Why?"

"There's the stink of tobacco smoke in here. You not getting it?"

"My sense of smell ain't what it used to be. Two decades of industrial cleaning products will do that to you."

Mary tipped her head and sniffed. "Yeah, I can smell it too. Kinda sweet. Not like cigarettes. Something else."

Leopold froze. The hairs on the back of

his neck prickled. He turned to Mary, his eyes wide.

"What is it?" she asked.

"I recognize the scent from before," he said. "We've come across it twice already, and I never made the connection. The smell isn't from cigarette smoke," he pulled out his cell phone and dialed a number. "It's from pipe tobacco."

Leopold paced the office. Mary sat at her desk watching, nursing a mug of coffee.

"Want to run that by me again?" she said.

"Think, think, think," he tapped his forehead with an index finger. "Tobacco smoke. The employee at the hotel reeked of it. At Biggs' house, there was an old pipe spilling ash all over the place. Then again in the cells. All three times, the same smell."

"Plenty of people smoke pipes."

"You ever run into three different guys

smoking the same flavored tobacco, all in the same day? Smelled like cherry to me."

Mary blinked. "Okay, maybe not. Still, it's not exactly groundbreaking evidence."

"Not by itself. But sometimes the smaller things lead us to the bigger things. You checked Biggs' file?"

"Yeah. Nothing much there we didn't already know."

"You got a photo?"

"The guy's got no record. No photo, no prints, no DNA. Why?"

"Call it a hunch." Leopold turned his cell phone's speaker on and lay the handset down on the desk. It was playing a Muzak rendition of "Uptown Girl." He pulled Mary's keyboard toward him and leaned in to get a view of the computer monitor.

"What the hell are you doing?"

"Just bear with me." He loaded up the internet browser and punched Biggs' name and address into the search bar. A few dozen relevant results bounced back, the top ones belonging to various social media sites.

"This isn't exactly the police database," said Mary.

Leopold ignored her and clicked on the top result. "Look. Recognize this guy?" He pointed at an image of a gaunt, aging man with black skin and gray hair.

"No, should I?"

"What about these photos?" He opened up the other search results, all pictures of the same man.

"You're kidding me," she said.

"Afraid not."

"The guy we spoke to in Brooklyn…"

"Wasn't Biggs."

"Shit."

"Well put."

"Then who the hell were we talking to?"

Leopold grinned. "My guess: if the pipe smoker was the inside man at the hotel, our fake Biggs was probably the one with the connections. You know, the middleman. He dispatched the real Biggs and waits at the apartment for the cops to show. That just leaves the brains."

"Don't get all Wizard of Oz on me," said Mary. "You're just guessing here. We're going to need more than that."

"You really think the fake Biggs, whatever

his name is, had the mental capacity to pull something like this off?"

Mary folded her arms. "I'm no psychologist. How would I know."

"You should learn to rely on your instincts. We both know there must have been someone else involved, someone who had working knowledge of the bank. Now that Creed is dead, our pool of suspects just got a little smaller."

"Not small enough. We need more to work with."

"I'm working on it." He picked up his cell phone just as the Muzak stopped and a man's voice came on the line. Leopold walked away from Mary's desk, just out of earshot.

"Blake?" The voice was strongly accented, maybe Puerto Rican.

"Yes. You have the information I need?"

"Your contact had to work fast. He had to drop a lot of important clients."

"He'll be well compensated. I trust you'll see to that. What have you got for me?"

"The wire transfer came from an account in the Cayman Islands. The corporation was a shell, as you might expect. We followed the trail through Geneva and then back west to the Caribbean.

"You got a company name for me?"

"Yeah. Umbrella corporation calls itself 'Plutus Inc.' I got a list of the directors and shareholders, though it's pretty short."

Leopold felt his pulse quicken. "Let me guess. Just two people? Share a surname?"

There was a pause on the line. "Yeah, how'd you know?"

"Let's just call it instinct. Text me the names." He hung up without waiting for a response and made his way back to Mary's desk.

"Let me guess: another lead?" she said, downing the remains of her coffee.

"You could say that." His cell phone vibrated and he held up the screen so Mary could see. "Somebody's been very, very naughty."

"Absolutely no freakin' way," said Captain Oakes. The captain stood up, slamming two heavy palms down onto his desk. "And who the hell is this guy?" he glanced at Leopold.

"Sir, Blake has been working with us on this case from the beginning," said Mary. "He found a lead on the killer. We need to get out there."

"And you want me to sign off on this? Based on what evidence?"

"We found data on Teddy Gordon's hard drive that suggests several accounts at Needham Brothers were being scammed. We also know that Gordon was killed because of his connection with the fraudulent activity. We also believe that Vincent Creed was set up to take the fall by another party."

Oakes slumped back into his seat. "You still haven't got any proof. This is all a hunch."

Leopold opened his mouth to speak, but Mary cut him off.

"We came across information regarding a substantial deposit made into Creed's bank account on the day of Gordon's murder," she said. "This payment was sent to make Creed look more guilty. We traced the accounts to an umbrella corporation."

"This is Plutus Inc.?"

"Yes, sir. 'Plutus666' is also the password that Teddy Gordon and his wife use on their home computer, the same computer where we found all the documents covering the scammed accounts at Needham. The Gordons did a good job of making it look like Creed had authored the files, but our tech teams managed to see past that."

"That's still not enough, Lieutenant. I can't get you your warrant without something concrete linking Melissa Gordon to the murder." He raised a chunky finger. "And don't pretend you followed protocol on this one, Jordan. I don't even want to know how you traced those accounts."

"But sir, we need to bring Mrs. Gordon in. And we'll need backup."

"Denied." The captain got to his feet again. "The DA is satisfied with the evidence against Creed and the medical examiner doesn't believe there was any foul play. Get some evidence, then you get your warrant. Play by the rules or don't play at all." He aimed the last comment at Leopold. "Now get the hell out of my office."

Leopold stormed ahead, leading the way back to the Mercedes where Jerome was waiting. Mary jogged to keep up.

"Hey, slow down," she said, putting one hand on Leopold's shoulder. "You heard the captain. We're on our own."

He stopped and took a deep breath. "It just seems that, no matter the environment, those who are most effective at setting up road blocks are the ones put in charge." He exhaled. "No matter. We just need to find something we can use. Why didn't you mention the fake Biggs?"

"What, and make us look even more incompetent? We need to go to Oakes and the DA with an ironclad case. That means we can't rely on anything you found on social media or anything your network of hackers managed to get hold of. We need to do this by the book."

"You're with me on this."

"Damn right," she said. "Everything I've seen today, Melissa Gordon is the only suspect that makes any sense. She and her husband must have been running the scam for years. I guess he grew a conscience."

"We need to get back inside her house," said Leopold. "If we can find something to link her to the fake Biggs or the money transfers, we've got probable cause. A full forensic sweep of her computer accounts should tell us the rest, along with whatever scams Needham was running. We can end this whole thing today."

"How do we get inside without a warrant?"

"Easy." Leopold smiled. "We just ask."

Jerome put his right foot to the floor and the Mercedes surged forward, throwing Leopold into the back of the passenger seat. A white van sounded its horn as Jerome steered over to the fast lane and cut it off. The bodyguard kept his foot planted and the irate driver was soon lost in the traffic behind them.

"You know, this is a terrible idea," said Jerome.

"I know you think so," said Leopold. "Though I'd appreciate it if you didn't run us off the road before we find out for sure."

"You should have waited for police backup."

"That wasn't an option. We can't get any support without evidence, and this is the only way we're going to find any."

"Have you at least told anyone at the precinct where you're going?"

"And risk them stopping us? No. We're well and truly on our own this time. Think you can handle it?"

"Assuming you don't do anything stupid."

"No promises."

Jerome grunted and undertook a slow-moving truck ahead, eliciting more honks of outrage. The exit that led toward Melissa Gordon's brownstone loomed ahead and Jerome took it, slowing the car down to a more sensible speed.

"We'll be there in two minutes," said Jerome. "Get ready."

The butler opened the door.

"May we come in?" asked Mary, holding up her NYPD shield. "We have a few follow-up questions."

The butler eyed the trio disdainfully. "Is Mrs. Gordon expecting you?"

"No. This is quite urgent."

"Please wait here." He closed the door.

"Once we're inside," said Leopold, "I'll need you to distract Mrs. Gordon while I take a look around. I'll make up some excuse. Jerome, I'll need you to stay with her."

Jerome nodded.

"What will you be looking for?" said Mary. "We already have most of the stuff off her computer."

"I'll know it when I see it. Just keep her busy."

The front door opened once again and the Butler waved them through. "Mrs. Gordon will see you in the drawing room," he said. "Follow me."

Melissa Gordon sat on the sofa, as before, with what looked like a gin and tonic in her hand. She sipped the drink as her guests entered and set the glass down on the coffee table.

"Detective. Mr. Blake." She nodded at Mary and Leopold before looking up at Jerome. "I don't believe I've had the pleasure, Mr....?"

"It's Jerome," said Leopold. "Just Jerome."

She smiled. "Please, have a seat."

They obliged.

"Detective, I heard about the incident with Vincent Creed. After what he did to my husband, I hope you'll forgive me for not getting too choked up about it."

Mary nodded. "We're all dedicated to justice here, Mrs. Gordon. I just had a few questions for you about Mr. Creed. We're hoping to get this wrapped up pretty quickly."

"Ask away."

"We are aware of some inconsistencies in the way Needham Brothers were reporting profits for their clients. Were you aware of anything like that?"

Melissa Gordon sighed and took another sip of her drink. "I haven't worked there in years. Teddy might have known, but I'm afraid I'm not part of that world any more. I can't help you."

"If you'll excuse me," said Leopold, getting to his feet, "do you mind if I use your bathroom? I'm sure Detective Jordan can continue in my absence. It's been rather a long drive."

"I suppose so." She put her drink down. "The door nearest the porch. I assume you can find your way?"

"I'll manage." Leopold brushed past the butler, who had brought in a tray of tea, and made his way out of the room.

He passed through the hallway and skipped the bathroom, opening one of the doors opposite. The kitchen lay beyond, pristine with shiny granite countertops. A large steel oven took center stage. Toward the back, another door led through to what looked like a utilities room. The smell of freshly laundered clothes wafted through, along with the quiet rumble of what Leopold assumed was a dryer.

He stepped into the small room, avoiding the basket of laundry on the floor. A side door led out to the garden. It had been left open. Leopold crouched and peered through the clear window of the dryer, watching the clothes tumble around inside. The machine stopped. Within, Leopold could make out several pairs of jeans, some underwear, and something else. The material looked different, cheaper. He shuffled closer and opened the hatch, looking in. A dark blue outfit had risen to the top, a clear insignia inscribed on the breast:

"New York City Department of Corrections."

Leopold closed up the dryer and got to his feet, feeling his heart begin to pound. The smell of laundry detergent was overwhelming, the thin breeze from the open door barely making a difference. There was another smell too; sickly sweet, like burned grass and…

Cherries.

There was a sound from behind and Leopold spun on his heels, hands raised in defense. A flash of movement caught him unaware and he felt something heavy connect with the side of his head. As he crumpled to the floor, Leopold saw the figure of an old man standing above him. The pain in his skull reached a crescendo and the man bent down.

And then darkness.

Leopold awoke with a blinding headache. He was sitting on something hard. As the pain subsided, he tried to stand – but found that he was unable to move. His body wasn't playing ball. Everything looked blurry. The room was dark, no windows. It smelled damp.

"Welcome back, Mr. Blake." Melissa Gordon's voice came from behind.

Leopold blinked hard and his vision returned to normal.

"I should have warned you about snooping around," Melissa continued. "Though I had hoped you would be smart enough to know not to go prying."

Flexing his wrists, Leopold felt something dig into his skin. He glanced down and saw he was tied to a chair, plastic zip-ties holding his forearms to the frame. Looking around, he could make out two figures in the shadows in front of him. Another voice came from his left.

"This was a dumb-ass move, lady." Mary's speech was slurred. "I'm a cop. You're going to have the entire NYPD hunting you down if you don't let us go."

Leopold turned his head. Mary had been placed behind him, at the edge of his field of vision. She was in a similar state, her wrists tied to a wooden chair. Craning his neck, Leopold saw Jerome sat a little further away, slumped in his seat, unconscious. His hands were also bound.

Melissa Gordon stepped out from the shadows and made her way to the front of the room. "Do you think I got where I am today without learning how to take precautions?" She smiled. "If you had any evidence against me, you would have brought your friends from the precinct. As it stands, I think it's a safe assumption you're here without any support."

"They'll work out what happened eventually," said Mary. "You should let us go. Now."

"If and when the police come knocking, they'll find nothing but an empty basement. My colleagues," she gestured toward the two figures, "took the liberty of going through your wallets. You'd be surprised what you can do with a credit card number. The police will be chasing you around the planet long after your bodies have rotted away." She smiled again. "I'm afraid there really is no way out of this."

"What did you do to Jerome?" asked Leopold, feeling his hands start to go numb.

One of the figures stepped into the light. Leopold recognized him as the fake Biggs, though he was now dressed in a smart suit.

"Your big friend didn't want any tea," he said. "So we had to be a little more forceful. He should wake up soon enough."

"You drugged the tea?" said Mary.

"I slipped a little something into your cup after Mr. Blake wandered off and got himself into trouble," said Melissa. "It seemed a more civilized alternative to a crowbar to the head. Please pass my apologies to your big friend when you get a chance."

"Tell him yourself," said Leopold. "I'm sure he'd love the opportunity to have a chat with you all."

The second figure stepped forward. A thick scent of pipe tobacco clung to his shabby clothes and he held an iron crowbar in one hand. "I bet he would."

"Look, are you planning on doing anything with us? Or is your evil plan to bore us to death?"

The man with the crowbar slapped Leopold across the face with the back of his hand. It stung like hell, reinvigorating the pain in his skull.

"James, calm down," said Melissa. "We're not animals."

The man called James grunted and stepped back, tapping his crowbar against his leg in irritation.

Mrs. Gordon continued. "I need to know what you found out about Needham. Tell me everything and I'll make sure this passes as painlessly as possible. Try to fight me and I'll let James and Bobby have their way with you." She glanced over at the two men. "And, trust me, you won't like that."

"Go to hell," said Mary. "They'll figure out what happened to Creed eventually. All they need to do is check the personnel records and they'll know the usual guard never showed. Do you think they won't figure it all out?"

"The guard we paid off will get his uniform and credentials back, any DNA evidence removed, of course, and nobody will be any the wiser. It's a pity you showed up when you did – James was due to make the drop before three." She glanced at her watch. "If the guard decides to cause problems, we'll deal with him then. Though I suppose that's not really your main concern right now, is it?" She took a step toward the door. "Now, if you'll excuse me, I have work to do."

There was a muffled grunt from behind. Jerome was waking up.

"Oh good," Melissa said. "The whole gang's here. James, Bobby – make sure our guests behave themselves." She opened the door and swept out of the basement.

"What, no bad-guy speech?" said Leopold. "I was really looking forward to that. I've got to say, you're all letting the team down."

James slapped him across the cheek again. It stung even worse than before.

"Cut it out," said Mary. "Just get this over with. Try to ignore him."

"Don't blame me," said Leopold. "I'm not the one being unreasonable." He looked up at James. "Just one question; why kill Teddy? He was your inside man. And the real Biggs, I'm guessing he's buried somewhere out in New Jersey? Or is that too much of a cliché?"

The fake Biggs, the man called Bobby, stepped forward. "Jimmy doesn't like to get involved in the details," he said. "He really just enjoys the action, know what I mean? Speaking of which, if you're going to play the smartass card, I might just let him have a little fun."

"It's a serious question," said Leopold. "We can give you the information you want. I have it all on a pen drive. If you tell me what happened with Teddy, I can tell you where to look."

Bobby sighed. "Fine. Just don't fuck with me, got it? I can make the remaining hours of your life very miserable, so don't tempt me."

"Yeah, I got it." Leopold turned to Mary. "You on board?"

"Whatever. It's not like you could make things any worse."

He turned to Jerome. "You awake yet?"

Jerome blinked hard and looked back at him. "Keep your voice down. I've got a splitting headache."

"You remember that time we were in Brazil?" Leopold said. "Happy memories, right?"

"Yeah. Happy memories."

"What the hell are you talking about?" said Mary.

"Nothing," said Leopold. "Just trying to take our minds off the situation. I guess this is the wrong crowd, so I'll get to the point." He looked over at Bobby. "Why kill Teddy? He was your meal ticket, after all."

Bobby folded his arms. "Don't mess around."

"I'm not messing around. I need to know what scam you were running. There was a lot of data on Gordon's computer. I need to narrow it down."

Bobby chewed his bottom lip. "Yeah, Teddy was a smart guy. But he was careless. He was the one who came up with a new market model — one that was more accurate than anything Needham had used before. Helped them make a shitload of cash by figuring out which direction the market was going."

"And you used this to bet against the poor performers."

"Damn right we did. And we managed to cover it up by moving losses around the balance sheets. Nobody had a clue."

"Let me guess," said Mary, "Teddy decided to call it a day?"

James snorted.

"You could say that," said Bobby. "He found something in the formula. Something nobody else could see."

"A way to scam even more money from innocent people?" said Mary.

Bobby laughed. "Innocent? You gotta be kidding. The market model Teddy had developed could accurately predict where the market was heading, but it was all based on the assumption that conditions kept stable. You know, that everyone paid their loans on time, kept buying shit they didn't need. They called it the 'volatility index' or some shit like that."

"And?"

"If the market conditions shift by more than fifteen percent in one week, the model is completely screwed. For a firm like

Needham, if they see a big change in the market, even over a few days, they could lose everything."

Mary shook her head. "How the hell would that work?"

"Investment banks trade on other people's assets," said Leopold. "They borrow money against stock they don't actually own, so if the deal goes south, the bank is on the hook for the difference between the market value of the stock and the amount they borrowed against it. If the volatility index gets too high, they start owing money. Hundreds of millions of dollars just vanish from their books and the bank has to stop trading. That means anyone who's invested with them risks losing everything. And I mean everything."

"Jesus. This is why I keep my spare cash in the mattress."

"Best place for it now," said Bobby. "He figured this out weeks ago. He wanted to come clean, wanted the bank to try and fix the situation before it got out of hand. Naturally, we didn't see eye to eye on that." Bobby grinned.

"You just saw a way to make more cash," said Leopold. "And now it's too late. Something this big is going to go public. You knew your days of scamming Needham were over, so you had no need for Teddy. So you decided to tie up any loose ends, which, I'm guessing, included Vincent Creed."

"Creed was the patsy," said Bobby. "He was too frickin' dumb to figure out what we were doing, but he made a perfect fall guy." He stepped forward. "Now, we answered your damn question. Tell us what we need to know."

Leopold glanced over at Jerome. The bodyguard blinked.

"Sorry, fellas," said Leopold. "I was hoping you'd keep talking a little longer. I actually don't have anything for you." He shrugged. "I figured you to be the talkative types. My bad."

Bobby looked at James and nodded. James cracked a smile. He walked casually toward Leopold, his crowbar in one hand. As he came within arm's length, he drew back the weapon and held it over his head.

"Last chance, smart guy," said Bobby. "Speak up, or we'll start with your shins."

Leopold sighed and looked over at Jerome.

"He ain't gonna save you," said Bobby.

The bodyguard shifted position in his chair. He shook his head.

"Looks like you're right about that," said Leopold.

"Hey, dumbass." James brought the crowbar down hard, aiming for the shin. There was a dull crunch as the iron bar hit bone and Leopold fought hard to hold back a scream. The pain was immediate and overwhelming, as though a firecracker had gone off in his skull.

"You're gonna answer Bobby's goddamn question or I'm gonna hack your freakin' leg off." James kicked Leopold's ruined leg with his right boot to prove his point.

The agony peaked. Tears streaming down his face, Leopold bit his lip and tried to clear his mind – an ancient meditation technique that supposedly made a person immune to pain.

It didn't work.

"You got any more wisecracks, asshole?"

James said, brandishing the crowbar. "Or we gonna start on the other leg?"

"Wait, wait," Leopold said, barely able to get the words out. He looked over at Jerome again. The bodyguard nodded.

"Last chance," Bobby said.

Leopold tilted his head up. "Go screw yourselves."

James smiled and lifted the crowbar. As he brought the weapon down, a grunt of pain from the back of the room caught him by surprise. He froze. "What the f —"

In one fluid movement, Jerome tipped himself backward, flipping over the back of his chair. He landed silently and drew up to his full height, his right arm hanging at a strange angle. He held the heavy chair out in front of him. Before James or Bobby could react, Jerome charged across the basement floor and swung the chair around, narrowly missing Leopold's head. The wooden frame smashed into James' shoulder, sending him tumbling across the room and into the back wall. His head smacked against the bricks.Bobby took a step backward, his palms raised. "Listen, buddy, don't do anything stupid. I got money." He backed up against the bricks. "I'm just a middleman, this was all her idea, I don't…"

He never finished his sentence. Jerome brought the chair around once again and smashed Bobby over the head, splintering the wood. Bobby hit the floor hard. He didn't get up.

"Jesus, are you okay? What the hell did you do to your arm?" said Mary, straining against her zip ties.

"Is he okay?" said Leopold. "I'm the one with a shattered leg." He winced as the pain in his shins reached an all-time high.

"I dislocated my shoulder. It's a little trick I learned when I was younger," said Jerome, pulling apart the remnants of the wooden chair. "I tried to teach Leopold, but he wasn't exactly a model student."

"Let me guess – Brazil, right?"

"Right."

"Doesn't it hurt?" asked Mary.

"Hurts like hell. I just choose not to be a baby about it." He looked down at Leopold. "Speaking of which, I assume you're not going to be able to walk?"

"Good guess."

"Let me out of here. We'll carry him," said Mary.

Jerome nodded and walked over to the edge of the room. He took a deep breath and slammed his dislocated shoulder into the wall. He let out a quiet grunt as it popped back into the socket.

"I'm ready." He flexed his right arm a few times. "We'll lock up on our way out. I assume you'll call this in?"

"With pleasure," said Mary.

"Then let's get out of here. We've got one more loose end to tie up."

Leopold hopped up the basement stairs on one leg, supported by Mary and Jerome. They reached the hallway and found it deserted.

"You going to call for backup anytime soon?" said Leopold, trying to ignore the searing pain in his shin. "It's about time the NYPD started pulling their weight."

"You know, for a genius, you really aren't that smart," said Mary. "They took our cell phones, remember? And before you think of anything else clever to say, just bear in mind I'm holding you up here."

"Try the land line."

"Hey, if you can find the damn thing, be my guest. But, in case you'd forgotten, we've got a homicidal she-demon to track down. Who knows what someone with her money has access to? She could be halfway to Canada by now."

Leopold opened his mouth to reply, but a loud noise cut him off. Outside on the street, the unmistakable sound of a large engine revving to the redline and the squeal of spinning tires.

"She sounds like she's at least got access to a car," said Jerome. "And unless you happen to know her license plate, we're gonna need to get moving." He lunged toward the front door, dragging Leopold and Mary behind him.

"Ow, Jesus!" Leopold buckled under his

ruined leg.

"Stop being such a girl," said Mary, trying to keep up.

Jerome charged through the doorway and on to the sidewalk, the others barely slowing him down. They reached the Mercedes and clambered inside. Jerome gunned the engine and slammed his right foot to the floor, wrenching the steering wheel to the side. The car executed a perfect donut, throwing up a plume of white smoke. Now facing the right direction, the bodyguard followed the tire tracks left by Melissa's car and took off in pursuit. After less than thirty seconds, he slammed on the brakes.

The traffic on Fifth Avenue was jammed, as usual. A sea of yellow cabs blocked most of the lanes and pedestrians weaved in and out of the stationary traffic. On the far side of the road, horse-drawn carriages filed in and out of Central Park.

"What now?" said Mary. "This car got a phone?"

"Just a Bluetooth connection," said Jerome. "Needs a handset to work."

"Well, then we're just shit out of luck. All

this fancy equipment and we can't even call for help."

"We'll just have to do this the old-fashioned way," said Leopold. He could feel the pain in his leg start to throb. He couldn't feel his feet.

"Great. Just great."

"Use your eyes. Look for anything out of place."

Mary looked out the window. "All I see is cabs. And those damn horses."

"Look harder."

"I'm looking, I'm looking. Wait..." she pointed. "There."

Leopold leaned over and glanced out the window. Across the street, a sleek Aston Martin convertible was parked on the curb. It looked empty.

"She's in the park," he said. "She's on foot. We need to move." He sucked in a deep breath and reached over Mary, opening the car door. "Come on, you're going to have to help me over the street."

"You're insane. How the hell are you going to catch up with her in your condition?"

"Just help me out the goddamn car."

"Jesus, fine." She slung his right arm over her shoulder and climbed out. Jerome turned off the engine and joined them, holding up the other side.

"Faster. That way." Leopold pointed toward the gates.

"Just shut up and hobble."

They crossed the road in a hurry, ignoring the angry honks and profanities from the frustrated drivers trapped in their cars. They reached the sidewalk and Leopold kept hopping, driving all three of them toward an empty horse and carriage. The driver looked up as they approached.

"We need a ride," said Leopold, slipping off his watch. "Here, take this. It's a Rolex."

The man stared back at him, wide-eyed.

"It's worth ten grand. Take it." He thrust the watch into the driver's hand. "Just drive."

The man nodded profusely and clambered into the buggy. Leopold, Mary, and Jerome followed, settling in to the uncomfortable seats in the back.

"Just head into the park," said Leopold, shouting over the noise of the traffic. "We'll tell you when to turn off. Go!"

The driver jostled the reins and they set off at walking pace.

"Move faster!" Leopold banged on the wood.

"I can't, it's the law."

"Screw the law." He felt Mary jab him in the ribs with her elbow and he winced. "Sorry. There's another five grand in it for you."

"I'm a cop," Mary said, taking over. "Don't worry about causing a scene. In fact, it would help us if you attracted as much attention as possible. And I'll make sure you get your money, don't worry."

"You're the boss." The driver coaxed the horse into a brisk canter and they picked up speed. Several people shouted abuse as they were forced to duck out of the way. The scenery whipped past outside and Leopold strained his eyes for a glimpse of Melissa Gordon. He gritted his teeth as the clatter of the horse's hooves reinvigorated the pain in his skull.

"How the hell are we going to find her in this crowd?" Mary asked.

"The park's full of tourists and joggers," said Leopold, raising his voice above the cacophony. "Use your eyes, like I told you. Everyone is wearing sweat pants or shorts, maybe a baseball cap if they're feeling dressy – it should be easy enough to spot a woman in two-thousand-dollar Chanel and four-inch heels." He pointed outside. "Look, over there."

Ahead, the path veered off to the right. Most of the pedestrians were heading in the opposite direction, toward what looked like a farmers' market. A brass band was set up in the middle of the lawn, playing some kind of Dixieland melody that Leopold couldn't quite make out over the noise of the horseshoes on the asphalt.

"Turn right here," said Leopold, addressing the driver. "And don't slow down." He felt the carriage tip to the left as they swerved.

"We're going the wrong way," said Mary. "She'll hide in the crowd."

"This woman is on the run – instinct is taking over. Trust me, she'll aim for the most secluded route out of here. And that's where I'm taking us." He felt the buggy hit a pothole and nearly slammed his head into the ceiling.

"I hope you're right. By the time I find a cell phone and get a unit over here…" She paused mid-sentence. "Wait a minute, what's that?"

Leopold squinted through the gap in the carriage, looking past the driver out front. Ahead, a figure was speed walking in bare feet, a pair of high heels clutched in one hand. A woman, dressed in expensive clothes. She turned her head as they drew closer. "That's her!" Mary shouted. She instinctively reached for her hip. "Dammit."

"We can do this without resorting to firearms," said Leopold.

"Says the man with the shattered leg."

"Your legs look pretty good to me."

"Flattery will get you nowhere."

He rolled his eyes. "You got this or not?"

"Relax," said Mary. "The bitch is mine. Just get me close enough." She assumed a crouching position near the doorway and knocked on the wood. "Keep it steady."

"Doing the best I can," the driver shouted

back. "Just don't mess up my cart."

Ahead, Melissa started to run. Her pace was surprisingly quick given her bare feet.

"Dammit, she's seen us." Mary grabbed hold of the door frame and tensed. "Can't this thing go any faster?"

The driver yelled something Leopold couldn't make out and he felt the buggy lurch as their speed increased.

"That's it. Keep her steady."

The noise of the horse's hooves on the path intensified. They drew closer. Mary was almost hanging out of the carriage, a look of intense concentration on her face. They were almost level with their target.

"Now!" Mary leapt from the buggy as they pulled within a few feet, her arms spread wide open. She landed hard, knocking Melissa onto the ground. Leopold heard a shriek of pain and saw the two women tumble over a grassy bank and into a ditch. They disappeared from sight.

"Stop the cab," he shouted. The driver obliged and Leopold almost fell out of his seat as the buggy screeched to a halt. His injured leg hit the wall of the compartment, sending more firecrackers off in his head.

"You all right?" Jerome asked, lifting his boss up under the arm.

"Yeah, I'll live. You haven't got any morphine on you, by any chance?"

"Over there." Jerome ignored him, pointing toward a wooded area twenty feet away. "Feeling up to some exercise?"

Before Leopold could reply, Jerome grabbed ahold of him and clambered out of the carriage, setting off at a jog with his employer in tow. They reached the grass in just a few seconds – despite repeated pleas from Leopold to leave him behind – and Jerome let go.

"Jesus, you trying to cripple me permanently?" Leopold leaned against the bodyguard for support. "Can you see anything?"

A muffled grunt and a rustle of branches answered his question. A few feet ahead, Melissa Gordon stumbled backward out of a hedge and toppled onto her back. A split second later, Mary burst out of the shrubbery and landed on top, pinning her to the ground.

"Looks like she's got it under control," said Leopold. "Maybe we should just stay here."

Jerome looked down at him. "And this has nothing to do with you not wanting to get your ass kicked?"

"Of course not. I just don't want to interfere with police business, that's all."

Melissa grunted as Mary held her arms down, preventing her from rolling over.

"You have the right to remain silent," said Mary, as her quarry squirmed and tried to spit in her face. "You have the right to an attorney. If you cannot afford one, the court will appoint one for you."

"I'll kill you, you little bi –"

Mary slapped Melissa across the face with the back of her hand. "You have the right to shut the hell up," she said, using her knees to keep Melissa from rolling away. "Any other dumbass thing you do say can be used against you as evidence. Now, do you understand your goddamn rights?"

Melissa snarled and tried to push Mary away, to little effect. She let out a scream of frustration.

"I'll take that as a 'yes'."

Leopold looked up at Jerome. "See, nothing to worry about."

The NYPD forensic team didn't take long to crack Melissa Gordon's computer passwords. After less than an hour, they had scoured the contents of her home and remote hard drives – giving Mary enough evidence to agree a formal charge with the DA over the phone. They found incriminating emails, client records, phone calls, money transfers, bank accounts. More than enough to guarantee a speedy trial. James and Bobby were brought in after a brief trip to the emergency room, and all three had opted to keep their mouths shut during interrogation.

Not that it made any difference.

Leopold and Jerome waited in the viewing room, watching Mary interview Melissa.

After some medical attention and enough painkillers to keep him from passing out, Leopold had opted to stick around. The Gordon family attorney was present, dressed in an immaculate suit and looking uncomfortable as hell. He advised his client to keep quiet. Leopold knew Mary wasn't going to let that stand for much longer.

"Understand me, Mrs. Gordon. This doesn't end well for you," said Mary, her voice clear as a bell through the interrogation room speakers. "You scammed people out of millions of dollars. Important people. You killed two men – your husband and Joseph Biggs. You tried to kill three others, including me. We have enough to push for a federal case here and there's only one deal on the table. If you play ball, the district attorney will recommend a custodial sentence. If not, it's the death penalty. The DA has a lot of pull, so his word goes a long way." She paused. "Do you really want to die, Melissa?"

The lawyer twitched. "Don't answer that." He looked straight at Mary. "Keep to the point, Detective."

"Fine." Mary leaned on the table with both hands. "I'll make it real simple. Before he died, Teddy Gordon discovered a financial model that could predict market behavior with greater accuracy. He figured out a shit storm is heading our way and he thought it was important enough to risk losing everything to make sure people knew about it. We want you to give us the formula. Tell us where you hid the files."

Melissa smiled. "The mayor is getting pressure from Wall Street and he wants me to help, is that it? Maybe you should tell me why the hell I should care."

"You should care because it means you get to live."

"I get to spend the rest of my life in prison? That's no kind of life."

Mary sighed and took a seat opposite. "You know what the lethal injection does to a person, Mrs. Gordon?"

"Detective," the lawyer said, "we can end this interview right now. Keep the questions relevant to the case."

"This is relevant to the case," said Mary. "I want your client to understand the ramifications of her decision. Or would you prefer she remain uninformed?"

The lawyer frowned.

"I didn't think so." She turned back to Melissa. "You'll spend at least six years after the trial waiting on death row. Your lawyers will appeal, of course, but the chances of a repeal or a stay of execution are less than 1%. You'll have to deal with the stress and disappointment of six years' of failed attempts to save your life." She leaned in close. "And when the day finally comes, you'll be led into a sealed room where your family and a few witnesses will be sat watching you through a window. You'll be strapped to a bed. Three injections will be administered. They'll stop your heart and lungs from working. And then you'll be gone."

Melissa didn't respond.

"Is that the end you really want? Six years spent waiting to die, in a cell by yourself? To die like a coward?"

After a moment of silence, Melissa turned to her lawyer. "Get out," she said.

"You can't be serious," the attorney said.

"Bill, I'm telling you to get the hell out. Go wait in the hall. Have a cigarette or something."

The lawyer left the room.

"You got something to say?" Mary said.

"Tell me the deal."

"You give us the market model. The DA recommends a custodial sentence. We put in a good word with the Bureau of Prisons, maybe get you somewhere with a little sunshine."

"And if I refuse?"

"You'll spend the next six to ten years locked up in the worst shit-hole supermax we can find, waiting to die. The choice is yours."

Melissa ground her teeth and stared at the floor. "It's not much of a choice."

"It's not supposed to be." Mary made her way to the door. "You have five minutes to decide."

"I'm guessing she caved?" Leopold caught up with Mary at her desk. "Although I wouldn't need to guess if you'd let me hang around to watch."

"Melissa Gordon's lawyer found out you were spying. He insisted."

"Fine, fine. Did you get the files?"

She held up a USB micro drive. "Damn straight."

"A job well done. What's the captain going to do with it?" He took the drive out of Mary's hand and held it up under the light.

"Those aren't for you," she said. "The evidence will be authenticated by a representative from each of the top financial institutes. If it's real, the decision will fall to the mayor. The SEC will probably get involved."

"What about the public?"

"I don't know; it's not my call. The captain seems to think if the general public finds out, there will be mass panic. You know, people rushing to withdraw all the cash from their accounts. That sort of thing."

"If what Teddy predicted was going to

happen actually does happen, maybe that would be the smartest thing to do."

"Well, maybe. Who knows? It's not our decision to make." She held out her hand. "I'll need that back."

"Heads up." Leopold smiled and tossed the drive back. "So, what's to become of Melissa Gordon?"

"The DA already signed the paperwork. She'll serve a life sentence, no parole. The lawyer wasn't happy."

"I bet he wasn't. He probably could have pushed for a better deal."

"You're right there," she said. "The mayor is practically salivating over this market model. She could have done much better. Thankfully, she's where she belongs."

"Wall Street always did support the mayor's policies on corporate taxation," said Leopold. "I'm sure they'll stand to profit from Teddy's work. Even if everyone else has to suffer for it."

"Like I said, not our call." Mary looked up at Leopold, a hint of concern in her eyes. "This bothers you, doesn't it?"

"What, the banks making cash out of

everyone else's misfortunes? I can't say it appeals to me, no. If Teddy was right and this storm is coming, all we're doing here is giving the financial institutions notice to dump their bad investments. It's delaying the inevitable. And who the hell gave them the right to come out of this any better?"

"What's the alternative?"

"If the news went public, we could recover. It might take a few years, but we'd get there. If we keep this secret and let the banks work their accounting scams, millions will lose everything. The economy will dry up and investment will move overseas. Other nations will start calling in their tabs. Entire cities will be forced to declare bankruptcy. Healthcare will be a mess. The government itself could shut down."

Mary sighed. "It's pointless speculating."

"I'm not speculating. I've seen the numbers in the Needham accounts. If Teddy's formula is accurate, and the DA seems to think it is, we've already reached the tipping point. It's already happening."

"Maybe it is." Mary stood up. "And maybe it isn't. But its not our job to make this decision. I'm taking this to the captain and then I'm going home. It's been a long day."

Leopold nodded. "Fine. I guess you're right. I'm going to go home too." He turned to leave. "Goodnight, Detective Jordan."

"Goodnight, Mr. Blake."

Leopold made his way to the exit. One hand thrust deep into his pocket cradled a USB drive, one that looked almost identical to the one currently in Mary's possession. But there was one key difference. Leopold's version wasn't completely wiped.

He allowed himself a smile. The mayor was not going to be happy.

The glow of the computer monitors hurt Leopold's eyes. It was past midnight and he was at home, going through the contents of the filched USB drive. The situation was worse than he had expected. Using Needham's numbers as a starting point, the math didn't lie. Any lingering doubts were now grim certainties.

There was a faint noise from behind and Leopold spun around in his chair. Jerome stood in the doorway to the study. He flicked on a light.

"You've been sitting up here in the dark for hours," he said, stepping inside.

"I hadn't noticed."

"You have a visitor."

"Let me guess…"

Jerome nodded. "Detective Jordan. She's not happy."

"She come alone?"

"Yes."

"Good, then I'm probably not going to get arrested tonight. Send her up."

"She's waiting in the hall."

"Then tell her to come through." He took a deep breath. "Oh, and give us a little privacy. This might take a while."

Jerome left. A few seconds later, Mary appeared. She looked pissed.

"Come in, take a seat," said Leopold, gesturing toward a set of armchairs in the corner. Mary obliged.

"You were expecting me," she said, as Leopold sat down opposite.

"I had a feeling you'd drop by, yes."

"You switched the pen drives. When we were talking earlier – you slipped me a blank one. Give it back."

Leopold leaned forward in his seat. "I would never do such a thing." He smiled. "But, if I did take Teddy's files I can assure you it would have been for noble reasons."

"Drop the bullshit. You've got millions tied up in the stock market; you're just covering your ass."

"On the contrary. Unlike most, I choose not to keep all my eggs in one basket. Sure, I might take a hit, but the impact will be minimal, I assure you. What concerns me is the effect this is all going to have on people like you."

"What the hell are you talking about?"

"Look, these analysts you've called in to help – what do you think they're going to do once they authenticate the source? They'll run on home to their bosses and spill their guts. The banks will dump their stock and tie up their capital somewhere else, meaning the people who invested with them stand to lose a fortune."

"So what? I don't invest in the stock market."

"No, but you can bet your ass the banks that control your savings and pension do," said Leopold. "Once they've been cleaned out, what do you think happens to your money? It goes right back into the pockets of the guys that screwed you over in the first place."

Mary frowned. "My money is safe. Not that there's much of it, but it's safe."

"It's happened before," Leopold continued. "In 1901 and again in 1929. You ever heard of The Great Depression? What about 1937, 1987, and 1989? Then again and again, every few years. And that's just in this country. Each and every time, regular people were hit the hardest – they lost everything. This time it's no different, except now we have a chance to warn people. Give them the ability to prepare for the inevitable, maybe make their lives a little easier. It's not going to be pretty, but it's a damn sight better than letting the banks have their way."

"What were you planning on doing, Leopold?"

He sat back. "If the media got hold of this information, we're all on equal footing. No special treatment for the banks. People can make arrangements, hopefully mitigate the impact. Maybe even keep their homes, keep their jobs."

"And the banks?"

"They're doomed anyway. The smart ones will bounce back, the others… well, suffice to say, there's very little they can do about it now. Giving them access to Teddy's work is only going to allow them to pad their directors' wallets before the doors shut for good. You really think they deserve to be treated better than everyone else?"

"What I think doesn't matter."

"Yes it does, Mary. You're a cop – it's your job to protect the people. That means not letting the bad guys win if you can stop them. That's what's happening here. Are you telling me you can't see it?"

Mary shifted uncomfortably in her seat.

"When the dust settles, the SEC is going to figure out what happened. But by the time they get enough evidence together, most of these bastards will be out of their reach. If we act now, we can at least guarantee some kind of justice."

"But the mayor…"

"Nobody will know the source of the leak, I guarantee it. None of this will be traced back to you. Melissa Gordon will spend the rest of her life in jail for her part in this – but it's time to cast the net wider. This is your chance to do the right thing."

"I don't know what the right thing is any more," said Mary.

"You do. You know it in your gut. These people we're talking about – they stand to make a fortune out of ruining the lives of millions. Are you going to sit back and let that happen?"

"You know, for someone with such loose morals, you're actually not completely rotten inside," Mary said, getting up.

"Thanks. That's the nicest thing you've said to me since we met."

"Don't get used to it."

"So what are you going to do?"

"The mayor is expecting the micro drive

with Teddy Gordon's files by three a.m. So long as it arrives on time, I don't think there's anything I need to worry about."

Leopold smiled. "I've got a feeling that won't be a problem."

"And if the media does get hold of the story, and it leaks on the national news, there really isn't anything I can do about it, is there?"

"Good," said Leopold. "Because I already sent the email."

Mary opened her mouth to say something but the words never came out. She shook her head.

"What?"

"You know, I was wrong about you," she said, heading for the door. "I take it all back. You really are a total asshole."

"Coming from you, that's almost a compliment." He got to his feet. "It was a pleasure working with you, Detective Jordan."

"Let's not make a habit out of it."

He took a step toward the doorway. "I had a brief chat with Captain Oakes. He agrees we make a good team. I suggested we might make use of our respective talents again in the future."

"What the hell are you talking about?"

"Nothing," he held up his hands. "I merely suggested that the Blake Foundation is looking for some charitable causes to support. And I pointed out that the NYPD annual fundraiser is just around the corner."

Mary clenched her teeth. "Get to the point."

"Let's just say, I've enjoyed our time together and I'm looking forward to our next case." He smiled. "Hey, maybe they'll get me a desk near yours."

"You've got to be kidding me."

"Is that any way to talk to your new partner?"

"Go to hell, Blake." She stormed out, slamming the door behind her. Her footsteps echoed through the corridors of the penthouse. He heard the front door slam shut. A few seconds later, Jerome appeared. He peeked his head through.

"How'd it go?" he asked.

Leopold pulled down a bottle of whiskey and a crystal tumbler from the bookcase and settled back into his armchair. He looked up at Jerome and poured himself a drink.

"Better than I thought," he said.

LATER THAT MORNING

Martin Parks always came in early. As a senior analyst at Needham Brothers, one of the top New York boutique investment firms, he was expected to put in a good deal of face time with the junior staff – and that meant beating them to the coffee machine. But today had been a little different. Instead of rising at six a.m. and getting into the office at seven, Martin had awoken to the sound of his cell phone going off at a little after four thirty.

Apparently, it was all hands on deck.

Forty minutes later, Martin had showered,

dressed, and caught a cab to the office. Now, just as the first hints of dawn were visible over the horizon, the senior vice president of trading was gathering his people and preparing to give a speech. That was never a good sign.

Straightening his tie, Martin made his way toward the mass of people, keeping his ears open for any snippets of conversation that might explain what was going on. As he passed by his boss' office door, he felt someone grab hold of his arm.

"Parks, get the hell in here." Ryan Gibbs, Martin's immediate superior, pulled him inside the room.

"Jesus, Gibbs. What's going on? This a fire drill or what?"

His boss' office was a mess of paperwork – client files stacked knee-high all over the floor, the desk a clutter of stationery and disposable coffee cups. The blinds were pulled shut over the plate glass windows, shutting out the glare of the city lights. "The whole floor's being let go," said Gibbs, collapsing into his ergonomic chair. "We're screwed. This is it."

"What the hell are you talking about? Is this something to do with Creed and whatever the hell he and Gordon were mixed up in?"

Gibbs fished a pack of cigarettes out of his desk drawer. He studied the pack carefully but didn't open it. "I'm talking about the end of the world as we know it," he smiled, a slightly manic expression on his face. "The shit's about to hit the fan, and guess where we're standing."

"Speak English, Ryan. What's going on?"

"It's going to be headline news in a couple hours. Our analysts have done the math. The board of directors has been here all night. Hell, I've been awake for thirty hours. The numbers don't lie."

"What numbers? What are you talking about?"

"A few months ago, we stumbled across a piece of information. It was a formula, a market model. Similar to the ones we use every day. Except this one was more accurate. We trialed it, made a freakin' fortune. Problem is, we didn't figure the market would shift more than a few points in a given week. We were wrong."

"Yeah, so what? Happens all the time."

"Not by thirty percent, Parks. Over the last month."

Martin's jaw dropped.

"You see what I'm getting at?" Gibbs said. "We used the new model to make smart buys. But we monitored the volatilities with our old model. Like some freakin' amateurs, we didn't notice until it was too late. We're leveraged up the ass, Parks."

"How bad?"

"Let's just put it this way – our liabilities will exceed the value of our assets if we don't unload everything in the next six hours."

"We'll get shut down."

"That's not the worst of it," Gibbs said. "If we try to unload our stock now, before the value tanks, people are going to notice. We'll have started a chain reaction."

"What are we going to do?"

"The board voted last night. That's why we're all here."

"They're going to dump the stock." Parks knew the answer already.

Gibbs nodded, staring intently at the packet of cigarettes. "Carson is going to brief you all. The first few hours are the most crucial. If we don't sell the bulk of our options before lunch, the buyers will catch on and run for the hills."

"They want us to sell the stock, knowing it's going to tank?"

"They're offering a bonus for the entire floor if we get this done on time. One mil each. Plus another mil each if we hit ninety cents on the dollar."

Parks leaned against the desk, his head spinning. "This is a lot to take in."

"Get your head around it quick, son. This is happening. Right now." Gibbs stuffed the unopened packet of smokes into his jacket pocket and stood up. "Fair warning. Get your head straight." He escorted Martin out the door. "And put on your game face."

Martin paused in the doorway. "Wait a minute. You said you found this new model months ago? Why are we only just figuring out the problem now?"

"Some people asked questions at first, but I guess nobody wanted to hear it. The signs were all there, but we were all too busy riding the high to notice. The alarm bells started ringing when one of our biggest accounts pulled out their entire portfolio. Happened yesterday evening, pretty late. Obviously, that got people asking questions. Made us look at the numbers properly."

"Which account?"

Gibbs leaned against the doorframe. "Blake Investments. They cleared out their stock options pretty much across the board."

"Guess they saw this coming."

"Yeah, and they left it 'til the last minute to do anything. Could have given us a heads up. Instead, the bastards hung us out to dry." Gibbs shook his head. "Carson's getting ready. You need to go. Good luck." He shut the door and disappeared back into his office, probably to sneak a cigarette.

Martin felt his throat close up. It was all over. Less than five years and his career was done – and two million dollars wouldn't last long. Not in this town. Not after the IRS took half and the rest went on the house. Not with school loans. Not with car payments.

Across the office, Senior Vice President Jack Carson stood with his back to the window. With the sun coming up behind him through the tall glass, he was surrounded by an aura of light. Like some kind of bizarre angel. Or a prophet. Or a demon. Either way, Martin knew, in the next few minutes everything was going to change – and he'd better be ready for it.

The senior VP held up both hands. The room fell silent. Carson addressed the floor. Martin listened, feeling the tension in the air. The words were carefully chosen but, somehow, hearing Carson say them had a deeper impact than Martin had expected. There were hurried whispers in the audience. Looks of shock and surprise. The curtain had been pulled back, revealing a sham – one that an entire office of people had given their careers to support. And their leader, the man charged with guiding them through the storm, was selling out.

The whispers grew louder and Carson finished. He looked around at the worried faces. "I can't pretend this won't be difficult," he said. "But we're survivors. We're warriors. You're the best of the best and I have every confidence in you." He waited as the murmurs died down.

"Are there any questions?"

THE END

LEOPOLD BLAKE
WILL RETURN

For updates about current and upcoming releases, as well as exclusive promotions, visit the author's website at:

Amazon Kindle Author Page:
http://amazon.com/author/nickstephenson
Kobo Author Page:
http://www.kobo.com/nick-stephenson
Apple iBooks: http://itunes.store/nick-stephenson
Nook Author Page:
http://www.barnesandnoble.com/c/nick-stephenson
Author Website:
http://www.nickstephensonbooks.com

ABOUT THE AUTHOR

Nick Stephenson was born and raised in Cambridgeshire, England. He writes mysteries, thrillers, and suspense novels, as well as the occasional witty postcard, all of which are designed to get your pulse pounding. His approach to writing is to hit hard, hit fast, and leave as few spelling errors as possible. Don't let his headshot fool you – he's actually full color (on most days).

His books are a mixture of mystery, action and humor, and are recommended for anyone who enjoys fast paced writing with plenty of twists and turns.

Author Page:

www.nickstephensonbooks.com

Made in the USA
Lexington, KY
21 September 2014